ONLY C
HAVE N

Jo Starobin was trembling, trying not to cry. "What if Harry only lied to me once in his life?" she said. "And he didn't tell me only to protect me from something terrible. What if the only lie Harry ever told me in his life killed him?"

Suddenly someone came running out of the kitchen. It was the long-haired handyman, looking as pale as a ghost.

"They murdered Mona Aspen last night, just like Harry," he said, his voice scratchy and broken, "they murdered her and hung her on a door."

Jo sat down on one of the kitchen chairs and stared straight ahead. The cats stared back at her. I think they understood . . .

About the Author
Lydia Adamson is a pseudonym for a noted mystery writer and cat lover in New York City.

A
CAT
IN THE
MANGER

An Alice Nestleton Mystery

by
Lydia Adamson

A SIGNET BOOK

SIGNET
Published by the Penguin Group
Penguin Books USA Inc., 375 Hudson Street,
New York, New York 10014, U.S.A.
Penguin Books Ltd, 27 Wrights Lane,
London W8 5TZ, England
Penguin Books Australia Ltd, Ringwood,
Victoria, Australia
Penguin Books Canada Ltd, 10 Alcorn Avenue,
Toronto, Ontario, Canada M4V 3B2
Penguin Books (N.Z.) Ltd, 182–190 Wairau Road,
Auckland 10, New Zealand

Penguin Books Ltd, Registered Offices:
Harmondsworth, Middlesex, England

First published by Signet, an imprint of New American Library,
a division of Penguin Books USA Inc.

First Printing, November, 1990
10 9 8 7 6 5

 REGISTERED TRADEMARK—MARCA REGISTRADA

Printed in the United States of America

PUBLISHER'S NOTE
This is a work of fiction. Names, characters, places, and incidents either are the product of the author's imagination or are used fictitiously, and any resemblance to actual persons, living or dead, events, or locales is entirely coincidental.

A
CAT
IN THE
MANGER

1

It was the day before Christmas and the day after my forty-first birthday. I was sitting on the floor of my apartment wearing jeans and a white fisherman's sweater, and Chinese boots.

I had just started my annual musing on the possibilities of peace on earth, goodwill to men, and all that, when the phone happily jangled. I picked it up swiftly. A deep voice identified itself as belonging to Mr. Harmon, from the Humane Society.

"Is this Alice Nestleton?" Mr. Harmon asked.

"Speaking," I replied, perplexed.

"Your cat has just been apprehended shoplifting in Saks Fifth," Mr. Harmon said, in a gruff voice. "Now, what the hell are you going to do about it?"

Before I could respond to the startling charge, the voice changed and I realized it was Harry Starobin. Old Harry was making one of his jokes.

"Relax, Alice," he said. "Your cats wouldn't know how to shoplift if they were plunked into an anchovy store. Is everything all set? We expect you."

"All set, Harry," I replied, and listened as he gave me my usual instructions on where to meet him. Then he hung up without another word, as usual. I replaced the receiver. I felt peculiar, as I always did after one of his rare phone calls. I felt like a child who had done something wicked. Why these feelings? Disgusted with myself, I changed gears quickly. After all, Christmas was almost here.

My Maine coon cat, Bushy, was asleep on the crocheted afghan draped across the maroon velvet sofa.

"Bushy, open your eyes," I said to him. "Here's your Christmas present."

One eye opened and closed. One paw twitched. Bushy was clearly not interested.

I opened the box and plopped his gift on the sofa beside him. "Merry Christmas, Bushy," I said, and gently yanked one of his beautiful ears to get his attention. Bushy opened his eyes, flicked his ear, and stared at the basketball. "It's not just any basketball, you silly cat. It's special. Look at the design."

I had found the ball at FAO Schwartz. There were raised colorful horrific designs embossed on it. The moment I saw it I knew Bushy would love it. It was a psychedelic sphere. It was a ball from outer space. It was a ball from another dimension. It would suit Bushy's whimsical nature perfectly. I could envision him whacking it across the room.

When Bushy didn't move, I pushed the ball along the sofa so that it rested against his nose. He sniffed it, yawned, and turned over so that his feet were straight up in the air like a dead bird's. Then he went back to sleep.

So much for that gift. Well, there was still Pancho.

I carried Pancho's gift into the kitchen. It was a small container of saffron rice. For some odd reason, Pancho had developed a passion for Indian food. But, then again, Pancho was a very odd cat.

I had adopted him at the ASPCA three years earlier, when he was about six months old. He was all gray. His eyes were yellow. His whiskers were rust. He was missing part of his tail and had a large ugly scar on his right flank.

Pancho seemed to have one goal in life: to escape from his enemies. With this in mind, he spent his days and nights racing through the apartment. He loved cabinets and bookcases and window ledges. The higher the route, the better.

Opening the container, I placed it in the sink. "Merry Christmas, Pancho," I called out.

I heard nothing for a moment; then a whoosh, and a second later I saw a gray blur flinging itself from cabinet to cabinet. Poof—there he was in the sink, his face in the rice.

I proceeded to unwrap the small barbecued chicken I had bought for dinner. Carla Fried was to arrive at six. Her visit was the nicest

Christmas gift I could have gotten. She was an old and dear friend, and I hadn't seen her in years. We had been roommates at college, studied acting together, moved to New York, and shared an apartment before I was married, and again for a brief time after I was divorced.

I was looking forward to her visit; I couldn't wait to talk with Carla about theater. How I craved theatrical conversations since I had become more and more isolated! As to the reason for that isolation? Well, I had gotten the reputation of being "difficult" and "quirky" and "kooky."

This translates into the simple fact that I no longer cared for mainstream American theater. I craved to act in something new and different, something on the edge. I was searching for an avant-garde theater that didn't yet exist, and in doing so I was alienating a lot of my old friends. I ended up working in a lot of wild one-night-stand productions by bold experimenters. And because the avant garde always attracts academics, I got some occasional work lecturing in university drama departments. Was it my avant-garde tendencies that had prevented me from "making it" as an actress? Who knows? My ex-husband used to say I'd never make it because I was too beautiful in a bizarre sense. I was every man's sexual fantasy, a Virginia Woolf character moving across a darkened wild moor wearing a see-through Laura Ashley dress. I was tall, golden-haired, painfully thin, and always available: half desirable woman, half taboo child. Or so he said.

I arranged the barbecued chicken on a paper plate and covered it with cellophane. Then I made a tomato-and-onion salad and set the table.

It was time to pack.

The cats and I were going to Old Brookville, Long Island, on Christmas Day. It was my annual three-day cat-sitting job for Harry and Jo Starobin.

Now, there are cat-sitting jobs and there are cat-sitting jobs. Most of them are just quick daily visits to cats in apartments whose owners are away on business or vacation. I collect the mail. I open the door. I feed the cat. I water the plants. I talk to the cat. And then I leave.

My annual cat-sitting assignment with the Starobins was different. At the Starobin estate, I slept in a small cottage with my cats, but spent most of the time catering to their eight Himalayan cats, who lived in the main house. The Starobins spent every Christmas in Virginia, leaving the moment I arrived on Christmas Day. It was lucrative, it was fun, it was a chance to get out of Manhattan. I had loved the Starobins from the first moment I met them—and I had met them under very painful circumstances.

A friend of mine who taught play-writing at the Stony Brook campus of the State University had killed himself. Or so the police told me. I didn't believe it because I had spoken to him about ten days before his death and he wasn't depressed at all. So I went out there, offering to clean out his apartment and office because he had no living relatives. What I discovered was not suicide. He had seduced a young male student. The student had murdered him and faked a suicide. When I found a series of letters from the student to my friend, I showed them to the police and he was questioned. He admitted the murder but claimed he was the victim of homosexual rape. A jury subsequently believed him and sentenced him to only eighteen months in prison on a minor manslaughter charge. My murdered friend had left two lovely cats. A professor at Stony Brook mentioned Harry and Jo Starobin as a couple who could find a home for the cats if anyone could. The professor was right. The Starobins found a home for the cats, and when they found out I was an actress whose main source of current income was cat-sitting, they hired me.

I pulled two matched Vuitton bags—gifts from an old admirer—out of the closet, carried them into the bedroom, and opened them on the bed. First towels, then shoes, then toilet articles, then cat food, then clothes, then some Glenn Gould cassettes, then the new biography of Eleanora Duse. I stopped. There was more to pack, but I was tired. I walked down the long hallway into the living room, lay down on the sofa next to Bushy and his psychedelic sphere, and fell asleep.

The buzzer woke me a few minutes after six. I jumped up and ran to the wall to press the release for the main door, accidentally kicking Bushy's new toy to the far end of the room, where it rattled a lamp. I was so dopey from being suddenly awakened that I wondered for a moment how a basketball had gotten into the apartment; then I was confused as to why there was no Christmas tree, until I remembered that I had stopped buying them because the cats ate the needles. It had been a very deep sleep.

I opened the door and stepped outside to see if the visitor was, in fact, Carla. If it was anyone else—and anything was possible in my neighborhood—I'd slip back inside to safety.

I leaned over the staircase railing and saw a woman on the third-floor landing. "Is that you, Carla?"

"No," she responded, "it's the ghost of Christmas past."

I kept watching her as she climbed the final two flights. Yes, it was Carla, but she looked different.

Carla Fried had been a flamboyant young woman. Her views, her clothes, her behavior, were always on the wild side. But the woman approaching me now was wearing a sober business suit, complete with, of all things, a tie. An expensive, sheepskin coat was draped over her arm. I knew that she was the executive director of an acclaimed theatrical troupe in Montreal, but this was a bit much.

My critical distance dissolved, though, as she rushed up the remaining stairs. We embraced like adolescents, laughing, weeping, squeezing each other with the strength of seven years of separation.

I pulled her into the apartment, picked up Bushy, and shoved the large red-and-white long-haired bundle against her chest. She hugged him. Bushy looked perplexed.

"And that's Pancho," I said, pointing him out in his attack posture on top of the table, dangerously close to the barbecued chicken.

"It's been too long," Carla said as she sat on the sofa. She was a bit stout, and her long black hair was in a demure bun. She wore no makeup except for eye shadow.

"Do you still drink Heineken Dark?" I asked.

"Always."

I went into the kitchen and returned quickly with a bottle, remembering that Carla had always preferred to drink out of the bottle.

The moment I sat down beside her, we started babbling about old friends, old events, old lovers; about men, theater, apartments, weather, politics, food; about Montreal and New York; about Camelot and Hades.

The outburst ended. Carla leaned back against the sofa and drank her beer. Her face was still beautiful, though I could see white in her black hair.

"Where are you staying, Carla?" I asked.

"At the Gramercy Park Hotel."

"Posh," I noted, and added, "you're welcome to stay here for a few days. I have to leave tomorrow morning."

"Why?"

"A cat-sitting job on Long Island."

"Yes, I heard."

"You heard?"

"I mean, when I was in Chicago last year, Jane told me you had to become a cat-sitter because your taste in theater had started to run to the lunatic fringe."

I laughed. "Cats and lunatics, Carla, I always loved them."

"It is very hard for me to imagine you on-stage in a painted leotard while a naked woman plays the cello and a borderline psychotic makes violent speeches in blank verse to the audience."

"Times change, tastes change," I noted, gesturing at her new mode of dress. She acted hurt, then flung a pillow at me.

"I also hear, Alice, that you're beginning to dabble in crime."

"You mean shoplifting?"

"I mean Tyler."

Tyler was my gay friend who had been murdered at Stony Brook.

"It was very strange, Carla. The police called and told me that Tyler had killed himself—slit his wrists. I had spoken to him only ten days before his quote suicide unquote and he was fine. Also, I knew that Tyler would never slit his wrists—he had an absolute horror of the sight of blood. Anyway, I went out there and found this very bizarre term paper by a student in one of his classes. Then I found a couple of letters. Then I put two and two together and went to the police. Anyway, it turned out that Tyler and the young man were lovers, and Tyler had paid the price for an affair gone bad."

"What a funny expression, Alice."

"What expression?"

"An affair gone bad."

"Well, that's what happened."

"Why did the police think it was suicide?"

"Well, Tyler's wrists had been slit open with a razor blade. The young man had drowned Tyler first in the bathtub and then immediately slit his wrists. It was ugly and ingenious. The police thought it was simply a familiar suicide with the usual progression: slit wrists, loss of blood, loss of consciousness, drowning."

"Grisly."

"It must have been."

"Tyler was a wonderful guy. Remember

that essay he wrote on Pinter's *Birthday Party?"*

"It was on *The Homecoming,"* I corrected.

"Well, anyway, you ought to visit me in Montreal if you like grisly murders. They're the specialty of bilingual societies."

"I don't."

"Have you ever been up there?"

"No."

"It's really very nice."

"Carla, you mean it's very nice to you, don't you?"

She laughed and nodded her head. "Even nicer lately. Did you ever hear of Thomas Waring?"

"No."

"He's a lunatic Canadian millionaire who thinks he can buy culture—buy anything. So he gave me one-million-five."

"Gave you?"

"Right. Gave me. Just like that. He gave me one million, five hundred thousand dollars to put on three plays next year. That's half a million a production. Do you know what that means to us? I've been putting on productions for the past three years with peanut butter and milk cartons."

"What are you planning to do with it?"

"The first production is *Romeo and Juliet*— next fall. And guess who we got to direct."

"Grotkowski," I quipped.

Carla laughed and clapped her hands, re-

membering the ferocious arguments we used
to have about the Polish director when he first
expounded his theories in America.

"No," she said, "not Grotkowski, but close.
Guess again."

"I give up."

"Portobello," she said.

"Giovanni Portobello?"

"None other."

"That's wonderful," I said. And it was. I had
heard Portobello lecture at Hunter College. He
was a tiny, misshapen man who spoke so quietly you could hardly hear him. But his ideas
were exciting. He believed, for example, that
Shakespeare was so familiar, had so entered
the popular consciousness, that his plays were
no longer theater; they were like sing-alongs.
His idea for presenting Shakespeare was to
maintain absolute historical integrity in the
costumes and language—while at the same
time changing radically one of the main characters, deforming that character, in a sense,
with bizarre costume or accent, to present the
audience with an intellectual jolt in the midst
of an otherwise standard production. Thus,
two of Lear's daughters would be dressed like
Berlin whores in an otherwise impeccably
Elizabethan production. And that was only
the beginning; he took his theories much further.

"I'm glad you approve, Alice," she said.

"You never needed my approval before," I
noted.

"True. But now I do. Because I want you in the play."

I didn't respond at first. It was something I had never expected. I felt strange, like a bug was crawling up my arm. "Are you hungry yet?" I asked.

She held up the bottle, indicating that she would prefer to finish her beer first.

I got up and walked to the far window. The street below was ice-crusted. The enormity of what had happened was beginning to become clear. My eyes flooded with tears. When I had been a young girl on a Minnesota dairy farm dreaming of the theater, all my dreams focused on one part: Juliet. There has never been and never will be another part like that. It is love and death and eros and repression all rolled up into one body. I didn't want Carla to see my tears, although she, of course, would understand them. How could one be an actress without being Juliet? Dialogue began to course through my head. What an astonishing gift Carla was making to me.

Then I heard her say, "The Nurse is a wonderful part, Alice. And you can make it very special."

The disappointment was so sudden and savage that I had to hold on to the window frame. Not Juliet for me. The Nurse. Then shame at my arrogance and my delusion flooded through me. Had I become demented?

How could a forty-one-year-old woman seriously believe that she was being offered the part of Juliet?

Turning toward Carla, I said in the brightest, cheeriest voice I could muster: "Let's eat now, Carla."

2

The Christmas-morning trip began poorly. Just as I was about to leave the apartment for the Long Island Rail Road, I realized that I could not handle two valises and two cat carriers. So I unpacked the valises and shoved the stuff into a large duffel bag I could carry slung over my shoulder, leaving each hand free to handle an imprisoned cat.

That duffel bag was an old friend. An aunt, one of those truly bizarre women one finds only in farm communities, had given it to me years ago when I had first enrolled in acting classes at the Tyrone Guthrie Theater in Minneapolis. It had gotten so beat up over the years that I had started bringing it to the laundromat once a year to get it bleached.

Penn Station was crowded with old women carrying shopping bags full of wrapped presents, clinging couples who seemed to have severe hangovers, foreign-speaking groups who sat on their luggage and proudly displayed Dunkin Donut paper bags, and hundreds of homeless people who had come in out of the nine-degree cold and were sprawled along the walls of the terminal in ironic celebration of the holiday.

I purchased my ticket, located the gate, and waited for the 8:22 to Hicksville. Bushy was beginning to act up in his carrier, as usual—scratching, meowing, complaining. He hated traveling. Pancho, on the other hand, was quiet, reflecting in his cage, staring straight ahead.

When the train pulled into the station and we were able to board, I chose one of the double seats at the end of the car so that I could place the two carriers facing each other. That quieted Bushy down somewhat—he could at least stare at Pancho when he was upset.

The train pulled out and I settled down in the warmth of the car.

Every time I went to the Starobins' I felt like a little girl going to collect a birthday present. The Starobins were a wonderful old couple. Harry was seventy-nine with an enormous shock of snow-white hair, a face so lined it looked like it had been ravaged by a garden rake, and a long, lean, often brittle body. He was a combative old man who loved cats and horses and butterflies and all sorts of strange creatures. He was a noted cat-show judge and he knew more about cats than any person I have ever met in my life. To watch him play with his flock of Himalayans was a rare, giddy treat. Whenever I thought about Harry Starobin for any length of time, I realized that deep down in my perfidious brain I longed for him as the good father/bad father I never had. It was disconcerting.

As for Jo Starobin, well, she was Harry's match. A tiny, hyperactive woman with cropped white hair, she gleefully attacked and argued with Harry in public and made up with him publicly. They were the only senior-citizen couple I ever met who seemed to be enjoying sex as much as they did when they were young.

As for the Starobins' estate, it was as though someone had plunked a nineteenth-century Russian farm into very posh Old Brookville. Their buildings were crumbling; their paint peeling; their carpets thinning; their horses old or dead; their livestock nonexistent; their heat cut off; their phone off the hook. They obviously were very land rich and very cash poor, and it didn't seem to bother them in the least. It usually took them six months to pay me in full for the cat-sitting job—but then again, their fee was very generous. Everything about the Starobins was generous.

Then I fell asleep. When I awoke I thought about Carla's offer to play the Nurse in her Portobello production. I had told her I would think about it, and I intended to. Noticing that Bushy was becoming obnoxious in his cage, I drummed my fingers on top of the carrier to comfort him.

Finally, an impersonal, bored voice announced, Hicksville. I gathered the duffel and the cat carriers, exited the train, and walked down the high platform steps, crossed the highway, and entered the parking lot where Harry Starobin always waited for me.

Harry was not there. I waited five, ten, twenty minutes, but there was no sign of Harry or his beat-up station wagon. I went over the instructions in my head to make sure I had done nothing wrong. Take the 8:22 to Hicksville on Christmas morning. Exit on the east side of the station. Go to the north supermarket parking lot across the highway from the station. That's exactly what I had done. Where was Harry?

At ten-fifteen I hired a cab to take me to the Starobins'. It wasn't easy because I didn't have his address. I knew how to find the place once I passed a certain gas station and then passed an overhead traffic light, etc., etc. Because of this, the cabdriver had to go slowly and make numerous detours. By the time we finally arrived, the cabdriver was so angry that he dumped me and the cats on the road right next to the Starobin mailbox.

I looked around. Everything was the same. I walked over the rise and stood at the beginning of the gravel driveway which led to the main house. The old long-haired handyman whose name I always forgot was chipping ice with a shovel. He stared at me, then went back to work. He was an odd duck. The decrepit barn was still standing to the left of the house, accessible by its own path. An ancient carriage horse was being groomed in front, steam

billowing out of his nostrils. The young
woman brushing him waved at me. I waved
back. That was the stable girl, Ginger, I remembered.

The cottage I stayed in was to the right of
the main house, reached by a narrow path. I
picked up Bushy and Pancho and started toward it. The path had been recently cleaned,
but there were patches of ice that had to be
negotiated carefully.

As I inched forward, I saw Harry's station
wagon was in the garage next to the main
house. So Harry was in. He must have just
forgotten about my coming out. The thought
infuriated me for a moment, but I mellowed
quickly. After all, he was an old man, and
when I reached his age I probably wouldn't be
able to remember even my cats' names.

I reached the steps of the small frame cottage with a brick chimney and left the two
carriers on the porch. The door was unlocked
as usual, and when I pushed, it opened reluctantly. It was an old cottage, low-ceilinged and
dank. As I walked in, I smiled. The Starobins
had cleaned it up for me. The floor was freshly
swept. The cot had obviously been newly
made, and even the pillows were fluffed. I
looked in at the small kitchen. They had put
in a new overhead light fixture and someone
had shined the chrome fixtures in the sink.

I walked back outside, brought the carriers
in, and opened them. Bushy flew out and leapt
onto the cot, rubbing himself against the

newly fluffed pillow. Pancho walked out slowly, evaluating the new terrain for possible enemies and flight paths. I picked up the duffel bag and laid it on the cot next to Bushy, ready to unpack.

Then I turned to shut the door.

Harry Starobin was there! He was right there—staring at me!

I laughed out loud in joy. "Harry!" I shouted.

I was about to take him to task, both for sneaking up on me and for forgetting to pick me up at the station, when I realized that I was staring at a corpse. Feeling suddenly weak, I sat down quickly on the edge of the cot.

Harry was hanging on the back of the door; a rope fastening him by the neck to the clothes hook. His eyes were wide open. His face was bruised and distorted. Blood spotted his white hair.

I could not look at him anymore. I grabbed Bushy tightly and buried my face in his coat.

3

Only the Christmas tree in the main house had escaped destruction. With all its ornaments and limbs intact, it stood in front of the fireplace, surrounded by slashed cushions, broken lamps, ripped-up carpets. Jo Starobin sat in her rocking chair, her face as white as her hair.

A detective from Nassau County Homicide named Senay stood in front of the tree fingering an ornament. He was holding his crushed wool hat in one hand, along with a checker-lined raincoat. Wearing a blue flannel shirt with a red tie, he was a tall, heavyset, oddly unbalanced man.

The Himalayan cats were wandering in confusion around the wrecked living room, sniffing the broken items. From time to time one leapt up onto Jo for a moment and then leapt off. She ignored them. What beautiful cats they were—essentially Persians with Siamese coloring—a profusion of long-haired colors dancing across one's eyes. They were looking for Harry.

Jo started babbling bitterly to no one in particular: "Where was I? I'll tell you. I was playing cards in Smithtown. Playing cards while Harry was dying! I was playing cards and poor Harry was dying!"

She started to rock furiously.

I closed my eyes. I couldn't stand watching her despair. My stomach was still queasy from the night before. I still had the shakes. And I could not get the image of Harry Starobin hanging grotesquely on that door out of my mind.

Detective Senay left off fingering the ornament and began to pace, making sure he avoided the cats. "Mrs. Starobin," he said, "we are going to need an inventory of valuables."

"What did you say?" Jo barked, staring at him like he was a lunatic.

"An inventory. We have to know what they took."

"What who took?"

"The ones who did this, Mrs. Starobin. The ones who murdered your husband. They were looking for something—money, gold, antiques. We need an inventory of what you lost."

Jo laughed shrilly and rocked even more furiously. Then she mocked him savagely: "Money? Gold? Antiques? We have it buried beneath the floor. We have it buried under the fireplace bricks. We have it buried under the bathroom tiles."

Then she collapsed in tears, and when she

recovered, she whispered to the detective, "We have no money. We have nothing but this place and our cats." She closed her eyes, stopped rocking, and dropped her head onto her chest.

Detective Senay looked at her, realized she was overcome, and walked over to me, standing next to the sofa. He had already questioned me about the night before: why I was out there, how I had found the body. "We need that list," he said to me in a low voice.

"I can't give it to you."

"But you're her friend. Talk to her."

"I'm her cat-sitter. I come out here once a year. Besides, she said they have nothing of value. From what I know of the Starobins, she's telling the truth."

"Listen, those thieves beat that old man to death slowly. They were trying to get information from him. They were looking for something. He died from a crushed skull inflicted by a blunt instrument; then they hung him up. If we get a list, we'll get them."

He paused, then leaned over me in a solicitous manner and asked, "How you doing?"

"Fine."

"Rough scene. You were in shock last night," he noted. He switched his hat and coat to the other hand and sighed warily. "What else can you tell me about Harry?"

"He was a wonderful old man."

"Yeah, I heard that. I mean something important."

"Like his shoe size?" I asked nastily. Senay's mode of discourse on Harry was beginning to irritate me.

One of the Himalayans leapt up beside me, rubbing against my arm. I scratched her gently.

"I never liked cats," Senay said, then asked: "You make a living doing this?"

"Doing what?"

"Looking after cats."

"More or less," I replied. He arched his eyebrows in disbelief. I was about to tell him that I was an actress as well as a cat-sitter, but was interrupted by a blast of frigid air from the front door.

It was the stable girl, Ginger. She shut the door behind her and walked quickly toward Jo. She was obviously agitated.

"Mrs. Starobin, Veronica and her kittens are gone! Vanished!"

She caught her breath and pulled at her thick, long red hair. She was wearing several sweaters, making her normal huskiness even more pronounced.

"I thought maybe she had been frightened by all the police cars and ran into the woods. But I've been looking for hours. She's gone! Vanished! Her and all her kittens!"

Her tone was pathetic: frightened, guilty, seeking absolution for something that she clearly considered her fault.

Jo opened her eyes and stared at the stable girl. Then she suddenly leapt up out of the rocking chair and screamed, "Shut up!"

It was such an explosive, violent exclamation that the Himalayans scattered to all points of the room looking for places to hide.

"Who is Veronica, Mrs. Starobin?" Senay asked.

Jo sat back down, shaken. "The barn cat," she mumbled.

Then she exploded again at the girl: "Harry is dead and you come in here crying about the barn cat. For all I know, she's under the barn with her kittens or on top of the barn. Don't you know Harry is dead?"

The stable girl could not face the old woman's rage. She turned and ran from the house.

"I have to go upstairs," Jo mumbled after she had left. "I have to lie down. I have to think."

She left the chair, woozy at first, then walking more steadily. We heard her clump up the wooden staircase.

Detective Senay sat down in the rocker. He seemed to be relieved now that Jo had left. It was rapidly becoming dark outside. The cab would pick me up at six and take me to the train station. I wanted to avoid the cottage until the last minute, but I didn't relish sitting there with the policeman. It dawned on me that I disliked him. But why? I had also disliked the police officers I had met in Stony Brook when I was out there concerning my friend's reputed suicide. I resented the way they went about things, I decided. They chose a script and they played it out no matter what. This one's conviction that Harry's murder was primarily a robbery seemed to me peculiarly at variance with the Starobins' obvious poverty.

Detective Senay was now rocking just as Jo had. The shock of discovering Harry's body was beginning to wear off me—I realized I was becoming confrontational. "I find the whole thing difficult to understand," I said to him.

He looked at me quickly, stopped rocking, and then played silently with his hat.

"I mean about thieves breaking in to find gold coins or Tiffany lamps."

"Who said gold coins? Who said lamps?" Senay asked.

"Whatever."

"These kinds of break-in murders happen all the time. This is a neighborhood of rich people. Break into any house in the area and the odds are you'll find something salable."

"They couldn't just have picked this house by chance," I said.

"Why not?"

"Because this is the one house for miles around that a thief wouldn't enter. It's run-down. It looks like a slum compared to all the houses around it." My comment irritated him.

"Look," he said, speaking to me very simply, as if I were some kind of idiot, "it could have been a random break-in or it could have been premeditated. We'll never know until we find them, and we'll never find them if we can't trace what they stole, and we can't trace that stuff if Mrs. Starobin doesn't give us that inventory list."

We sat together in silence until Jo came down again. I said good-bye to her, nodded to the detective, and started back to the cottage to collect the cats and the luggage. The cab would wait for me on the main road.

When I reached the door of the cottage, I heard the most peculiar sound. At first I thought it came from within—that the cats were carrying on. But it came from outside, from the rear of the cottage, in the clump of pin oaks. It sounded like a hurt, crazed animal.

What could it be? I didn't really want to find out. There was nothing about the cottage inside or out that I could approach without fear. Harry's corpse had guaranteed that. But I couldn't leave it either. The sound was too pathetic.

I started moving around the cottage carefully, quietly. The wind was picking up, scattering dry twigs. The sounds stopped. I stopped. They started again.

When I turned the corner, I realized what I was hearing—someone weeping so hard that the whole body seemed to resonate. It was the stable girl, Ginger. Her hands were braced against the back of the cottage as if she were too weak to stand without support.

She heard me approaching, but she couldn't compose herself. I stopped two feet or so away. I had never seen anyone weep like that.

I didn't know what to do. But I had to do something. I placed my hand on her wrist and squeezed. "They'll find the kittens, Ginger," I said.

She screamed at me, gasping for breath: "Fuck the kittens. I hate the kittens," and then she just collapsed.

I knelt beside her, trying to cradle her body against me. But she was thrashing about.

"Harry," she started to whisper again and again with a desperate persistence: "Harry, Harry, oh God, Harry."

Then she grabbed me and held on. We huddled there on the ground in the dark cold. Finally, she started recovering her composure.

Her behavior perplexed me. Why had she sought out an isolated place to weep? Jo was weeping. Weeping was acceptable; almost demanded. A much-loved man had been murdered. Obviously Ginger didn't want someone to see her weeping. But who? And why?

I helped her up. She couldn't speak, but merely nodded her thanks. It had to be Jo Starobin from whom she wanted to hide her horrendous grief. But why hide grief from Jo? Jo, above all, would understand.

Unless, of course, it was the grief of a lover.

As I walked Ginger to the front of the cottage, holding tightly to her arm, I realized with astonished certainty that this young girl and old Harry Starobin had been lovers.

4

At six in the morning, four days after Harry's murder, I heard from Jo Starobin again. Her call woke me from a deep sleep. As usual, at that time in the morning my apartment was freezing. As usual, Bushy was on the pillow next to me. Pancho was somewhere else, plotting his next escape attempt.

"Am I speaking to Alice Nestleton?"

That's what I heard when I picked up the phone. For some reason, in my sleepy state, it seemed to be one of the funniest things I had ever heard. Is this Alice Nestleton? Is this Joan of Arc? Is this Ti Grace Atkinson?

My laughter irritated the caller.

"Maybe I have the wrong number. I'm looking for Alice Nestleton."

"This is she," I answered, which seemed even funnier.

"Alice, it's Jo, Jo Starobin."

I felt stupid and ashamed. "Jo, I'm sorry. I just got up."

"I'm sorry to call so early. I'm in Manhattan, at the Hotel Tudor."

"On Forty-second Street?"

"Yes. Can you meet me this morning? At nine o'clock?" Her voice was hurried, demanding, hopeful.

Did I have any appointments? I couldn't remember any. I said that I would meet her.

"At the Chemical Bank," she said, "on the corner of Fifty-first Street and Third Avenue."

And then she hung up abruptly. I listened dumbly to the dial tone. Then I replaced the receiver and pulled the blankets around me. I was glad she had called. In the days since the murder I had tried desperately to think of some gesture or some way to tell her that I understood her grief. But nothing had seemed authentic enough, so I had done nothing—not a card, not a flower, not a call; nothing. Now, at least, I could be of some assistance. Maybe she wanted a shoulder to cry on. Maybe she wanted to tell me about Harry.

The phone rang again as I was dressing. It was Carla Fried.

"Are you back in Montreal?" I asked.

"No," she laughed, "Atlanta. Something came up. You know how it is with us famous theater people."

I hoped she wasn't going to press me about the part. I had other things on my mind.

"Look, Alice, I just wanted to tell you how wonderful it was seeing you and talking to you. I could talk to you for five days straight."

"Like old times," I said.

"Like old *good* times," she corrected, and

then said breathlessly, as if she was in a great
hurry, "Look, Alice, I don't know my sched-
ule. But if I pass through New York on my
way back, let's get together again."

I agreed. She hung up. Given the horror of
what had happened in Old Brookville, the idea
of my old friend Carla Fried dashing across
the country like a Hollywood version of a
theatrical entrepreneur seemed somewhat
frivolous.

I left my apartment, which is on Twenty-
sixth Street and Second Avenue, at eight
o'clock and walked slowly uptown. It was one
of those peculiar days between Christmas and
New Year when people seemed exhausted and
confused. A black teenager's boom box blared
some rap song that I foolishly thought for a
moment was an updated version of a Christmas carol.

I arrived at the bank around eight-forty-five.
Jo was standing there like a lost child, wearing a pair of old-fashioned earmuffs.

"We're early. We'll wait," Jo said.

It had never dawned on me that Jo really
wanted to go into the bank. I had thought it
was just a place to meet. But she obviously
was waiting for the bank to open. She looked
terrible—exhausted, nervous, confused. She
grabbed hold of my arm and held it.

When the bank doors opened, I followed Jo
inside and down a flight of stairs to a large
glass door locked obviously from the inside.

Jo rang a buzzer. The door opened and an elderly man wearing a gray jacket with a white carnation ushered us into the safe-deposit-vault area. Jo signed a slip and handed him a key. He vanished into the vault area and returned quickly with a large steel box, which he carried toward the rear of the room, Jo and I following.

We entered a small carpeted room with three chairs and a long table. He set the box down on the table and left the room without a word, closing the door behind him.

We just sat there and stared at the box. I didn't understand what we were doing there.

Finally Jo said, "I was down here yesterday to pick up Harry's will. Do you know that it was the first time in fifteen years I had looked in the safe-deposit box?"

"I never had one," I replied.

"Oh, they're quite nice, quite functional," Jo replied, and I caught a hint of sarcasm. Or was it bitterness?

"Would you please open the box for me, Alice?" she asked.

I leaned over, disengaged the latch, and lifted the heavy steel top. I straightened up quickly. Inside was more money than I had ever seen in my life. The box was stuffed with packs of hundred-dollar bills held together by rubber bands.

"Do you see it? Do you see it?" she asked in an hysterical whisper.

I passed my hand over the top layer, gingerly touching the money.

"Three hundred and eighty-one thousand dollars, Alice. Three hundred and eighty-one thousand! Where did Harry get all this money? Why didn't he tell me? How did he get the money?"

I shook my head. I couldn't even fantasize an answer.

"Do you know what I think, Alice? I think this is why he was murdered. I think this is why." She slammed the top of the box shut.

"Have you told the police?" I asked.

"No," she replied abruptly. She paused, staring at me, and then said, "I was going to tell them. But I thought about it. And now I'm not. Look, Alice, Harry and I didn't have a dime. Everything was mortgaged. We owe everybody. And I think Harry wanted this money to pay off our debts and give us the farm free and clear. Harry would want me to use the money for that. Whatever he did to get the money, I know he did it for us, and the cats, and the carriage horses. This was his Christmas present to all of us, and if I tell the police, they're going to impound the money or do something like that or take half of it for taxes. Do you see what I mean, Alice? I'm not being a thief. I know what Harry would have wanted."

"He never said anything about this, Jo?" I asked skeptically.

"Never. Not a word. I swear, Alice. Never,

never, never." Then she stood up, placed her palms on either side of her head, saying, "Do you think he robbed a bank? Poor Harry. Maybe he robbed a bank because he wanted a Christmas present for all of us. I said to him about a month ago, when we couldn't pay the heating-oil people, that I was so sick of it I wanted to die. He just kissed me on the forehead and said I shouldn't get upset."

She started to cry, then caught herself and clapped her hands together like she was a teacher and I was a boisterous kindergarten pupil. "I want a cup of coffee, Alice. Can you take me for a cup of coffee?"

Five minutes later we were sipping coffee from containers in the Citicorp Atrium. On the walk over, Jo had kept chattering nervously: "Have you ever seen so much money?" "Did you see the way it was packed?" "All those rubber bands. All those hundred-dollar bills!"

As hundreds of children raced through the atrium, brought there to view the Scandinavian Christmas decorations, which hung from ceiling to floor, Jo sent me for another cup of coffee and for something sweet. I returned with a raisin Danish. She began picking the raisins off with a plastic spoon.

"Now, listen to me, Alice Nestleton," she said. "I called you for a reason, not just to stare at money or buy me coffee. I know a lot of people think I'm a little crazy."

"No one thinks that, Jo. Everyone I ever met

out there loves you, Jo, just like they loved Harry," I replied, and I meant it.

"Well, I know why Harry was murdered now. It was for that money, right? But it doesn't mean a thing unless we know how he got the money. Because if we know how he got it, we'll know who wanted it. And I know how to find out who murdered poor Harry. He never threw anything away. He saved letters and bills and business cards and cat-show programs and scraps of paper. He saved everything and it's all there and all I have to do is go through it all. But I can't do that, Alice. I can't see too well. And I don't have patience. But you can come out for a few weeks, Alice— and your cats too—you can help me. I'm going to pay you two hundred dollars a day. And we can find out what Harry did and who murdered him. Can't we do that?"

I didn't know what to say. If the killers had been after Harry's cash, why hadn't they guessed it was in a bank vault? And why kill him? Only he could get the money out. They would want him alive to extricate the cash for them. No, it had to be something else.

Poor Jo! She looked so vulnerable sitting there, those ridiculous earmuffs all twisted up on the side of her head. I wondered what kind of old woman I would be if I ever reached her age.

"You don't have to tell me right now. Take your time, Alice. You can call me at the hotel."

* * *

When I have to think—I mean really sit down and think—I like to sit in front of my mirror. It's a sort of reverse narcissistic game I play that gets my brain working.

An hour after leaving Jo, I was staring at myself in the mirror. As usual, I found my appearance baffling. As usual, there was the confusion over which one of us was the audience.

Two plum offers had suddenly appeared. Should I play the Nurse in *Romeo and Juliet?* I no longer had any allegiance to classic theater. I was interested only in the far reaches of the envelope. I would rather be paid nothing to stand onstage stark naked reciting Baudelaire's reflections on whores, while eating a tangerine. No, I decided the theatrical offer was not pressing. It could wait.

Jo's offer was more pressing. The money was certainly tempting. Yet the idea of spending a few weeks with Jo Starobin was unappealing. The woman's grief was so pervasive that those around her simply couldn't escape it.

I stared at my hair. There was a lot of gray in the golden flax these days. My eyebrows were getting paler. The face in the mirror was impassive. I had never understood how people could characterize me as beautiful. My face was too thin—wan, as they used to say. I chuckled. I squared my shoulders. It was my posture that they had always confused with beauty. When I had been younger and walked into a room, I always created a stir. Stage presence.

I saw a blur move across the upper-right-hand side of the mirror. Then it stopped. Pancho was on top of the bookcase, next to the volumes of the *Tulane Drama Review*, one of which contained a picture of me performing in a one-act play at the Long Wharf Theater in New Haven.

Pancho's image was staring at me.

Without turning, I said, "Look as long as you want, Pancho."

He didn't answer. His half-tail was moving back and forth. His face was set.

"Oh, Pancho, why can't you ever relax? Why can't you ever play?"

No response. I longed at that moment to gather Pancho in my arms, but I remained seated. Pancho was a good teacher. His reserve, his peculiar sense of constant danger, made him a good teacher. Some people, some animals, could only be loved from a distance. Intimacy was impossible.

"Run, Pancho, run," I whispered to his image in the mirror. All he did was lift a foot and begin to groom it with his tongue. He would flee when he was ready.

I touched the mirror with my fingers, running them along the glass just as I had run my hands along the top of the money in the safe-deposit vault.

Jo's offer had been financially generous.

Two hundred dollars a day for two weeks ran to twenty-eight hundred dollars tax-free. That was a lot of cat food. Plus, the offer came at a good time. The first few weeks of the New Year were always depressing and empty of possibilities.

I smiled at myself in the mirror, a bit grimly. An old lover of mine had once told me that my smile was terrible; it was totally dishonest. I made a face. It was irritating but true that I often evaluated myself by what men I had known told me. Why did I believe them? I was too old for such nonsense.

A blur flashed across the mirror. Pancho was on the move.

I picked up a hairbrush and balanced it in my hand. It was a beautiful tortoiseshell brush with fine stiff bristles.

It was perfect for a head of thick hair like that stable girl had, I realized. Ginger had that gorgeous thick red hair. I remembered her with a sudden flash of hatred. My reaction was so bizarre, I stood up and walked away from the mirror. I sat down on the bed.

Why wasn't I feeling compassion for that girl, like I felt for Jo?

Ginger's grief had been stupefying. She had wept like someone who had lost everything. No, I realized, I did not hate her. I was jealous of her.

Why? Because Harry and she had been lovers!

Agitated, I left the bed, walked into the hallway, and then back to the bedroom.

Why was I jealous? Harry had been a surrogate absent father—kindly, eccentric, wise, comforting, *safe*. Was that the way I had really felt? No, I wanted to be in that girl's place. I wanted to mourn Harry as a lover.

I walked quickly down the hallway and into the living room. I scooped Bushy off the sofa and hugged him. He accepted the attention stoically.

"Bushy!" I called his name. He looked past me. I whispered into his ear, "You knew all along I would accept Jo's offer, didn't you? You knew it all along."

I lay down on the sofa, still holding him. There was no reason not to go back out there. I had discovered Harry's corpse. Why shouldn't I discover his murderers? What else were fantasy lovers for?

5

I left the cottage and walked hastily toward the main house. It was a wet, cold morning. The trees were threatening—naked, precarious, hovering over the property. I had no qualms about leaving the cottage because Pancho and Bushy had settled in nicely; although Pancho seemed perplexed at the lack of space in which to flee. He would have to develop a circular flight.

"Is that you, Alice?" Jo cried out from the kitchen when I entered.

Then she appeared in a ludicrous outfit. She was wearing a huge leather apron with deep pockets—like a blacksmith would wear—and around her neck was an enormous and very frayed kitchen towel. "You arrived just in time. I was making eggs," she said.

Her ancient kitchen table with its splintered wooden legs was piled with utensils and condiments, as if she was embarking on a major feast rather than a modest breakfast for two. She pointed to the clutter and said, "Harry always made the eggs. He used to say I didn't know how to fry them, scramble them, poach them, or even boil them. I never knew whether he was serious or not. Well, here I am, without Harry, and I'm going to make eggs. How would you like them, Alice?"

"Scrambled would be fine, Jo," I replied, sitting down at the table to watch her. It was zany, but that was one of the Starobins' most wonderful qualities: they always did things outlandishly.

Carefully, almost painfully, she broke five eggs in a saucer and then proceeded to whip them with a flourish, her blacksmith's apron continually getting in the way. When the scrambling was finished, she collapsed suddenly into a chair.

Two of the long-haired Himalayan cats leapt onto her—one on her lap, one on her back. Two more leapt on the table, prowling, inspecting. One nuzzled my foot. In the space of seconds, they all changed places in a macabre, swift game of musical chairs. Then they all ran from the kitchen as if they had sensed the ghost of Harry Starobin in the eggs. It was very sad. The cats seemed lost.

"God, I'm tired," Jo said, and then she broke into tears, choked them back, and stood up. "It's doing all those stupid things around the barn. I find it very, very hard. I hadn't mucked out a stall in ten years."

"What about Ginger?"

"Oh," she said with an airy flip of her whisk, which she had not relinquished after scrambling the eggs, "she left two days ago."

"Left? Where did she go?"

"I don't know. How should I know? She quit."

This was totally unexpected. I had thought the girl would stay on, if only to assuage some of her guilt for being Harry's lover.

"Did she say why?"

Jo started to butter a pan, making a lot of clanking noises at the enormous black range. I could see that she had put much too much butter into the pan.

"She didn't say why," Jo replied, gazing thoughtfully into the melting butter, "but I know why. She was sad. Harry was like a father to her. And she was sad about the calico barn cat, about Veronica. That's stupid, though. Barn cats always vanish—sometimes for months. Especially when they have kittens. Veronica is probably living with some neighbor down the road now, quite happy, and one day she'll just meander back. I told her what Harry used to say—that cats can predict earthquakes and other natural disasters long before they happen. And they vanish. I told Ginger that maybe Veronica knew that Harry was going to be murdered so she ran away with her kittens. But Ginger wouldn't stay."

Jo poured the eggs into the sizzling butter and leaned over the pan, her tiny frame dwarfed by the gigantic apron.

I would have to tell her that Ginger was Harry's lover, I realized. Of course, I had no proof of it, only very circumstantial evidence—desperate weeping in seclusion. But Jo and I could go nowhere unless at the outset we were totally honest, unless even informed intuition was honored. What was the point of any other approach?

She finished the eggs triumphantly and shoveled them onto the plates. Then she stepped back and shook her head. She had been so engaged with the eggs that she had forgotten everything else—bread, coffee, juice. Clumsily she covered the eggs on the plates and proceeded to make the remains of the meal. I should have helped, but I didn't. My mind was on how to approach the matter of Ginger and Harry Starobin.

Finally we ate, amidst the clutter, the eggs cold, the coffee weak, the bread stale.

When we were finished, Jo heaved a great sigh, as if she could not handle such an assignment again for a long while.

"Jo," I said, moving my chair closer to her, "I want to tell you something, but I don't really know how to go about it. I don't want to . . ." I stopped, at a loss for words.

"Then just tell me. I'm too old for nonsense, Alice. Don't you know that?"

I started to pile the plates, moving the condiments, gathering the dregs. "I think Ginger was having an affair with Harry."

"You think?"

"Yes. I think so."

"What do you want me to say?"

"What you know."

"I knew nothing of that," she said quickly, and began to clear the table.

"Jo, please, tell me what you know."

"Listen, Alice," she said, leaning against the sink, undoing the leather apron, "Harry was a very strange and wonderful man. He had many enthusiasms. Sudden enthusiasms. He would suddenly take a fancy to a person or an animal or a house—anything—and he would give that person or thing his total attention. He would do anything for people. A lot of people loved him. He loved a lot of people. But that Harry and the girl were sleeping together . . . well, no, I don't think so."

"Why not?"

"Because," she said, flaring angrily, "he would have told me."

"He didn't tell you about the money," I noted.

She had removed her apron and the towel, and began looking out the window, anything to avoid looking at me. Obviously she was trying to control her anger toward me.

"Do you want more coffee?" she asked stiffly. I shook my head. It was a very awkward moment. But I had done the right thing. I wasn't there to be a nursemaid.

"Look how gloomy it is out," she exclaimed, and shook her head as if the world was truly deranged.

"Maybe it'll clear up," I said tritely. "Maybe the afternoon will be better."

"I want to show you his files," she said abruptly. Relieved, I stood up. We walked together through the long kitchen and into an adjoining storeroom. Flanked by two small, filthy windows, a door at the far end led out into the yard.

The room was filled with cardboard cartons piled on top of each other. Between the cartons, in haphazard fashion, lay ropes, old boots, pots and pans, and piles of clothing that obviously hadn't been worn in years. Jo opened one carton and beckoned me to peer inside. It was filled with letters and correspondence of all kinds. On the side of the box was written in now-fading Magic Marker: "1984."

"Everything," she said, "he kept everything. It's all here. Harry never threw anything away, not his letters, not his bills . . ."

I saw that each carton had a year written on the side. There were also many large manila envelopes among the cartons, and these too had dates. But there was no order to them at all. They just lay randomly in that damp, cold room, illuminated only by a single overhead light bulb.

"I can bring it all out to the living room and you can work there when you are ready," Jo said tentatively. We both realized that we had embarked on a problematic task—it could all be worthless as a key to his death. And even if we found one or two or three pieces of paper mentioning the source of Harry's newfound wealth, how were we to recognize them when they passed through our hands?

"Look," Jo said, pulling a sheaf of photographs from a carton marked "1975." She flipped through them and held up one for me to see. "That's Harry and some friends of his in Vermont. Look at the porch of that hotel . . . so lovely . . . do you see the rocking chairs?"

She didn't wait for an answer. She pushed the photos back into the carton. She was trembling and trying not to cry.

"I'll start on it tomorrow, Jo," I said, wanting to get her out of this room that was causing her such pain.

She made a motion with her hand for me to stay put. Then she said, "What if Harry lied to me only once in his life? About the money. And he didn't tell me only in order to protect me from something terrible. What if the only lie Harry ever told me in his life killed him?"

There was nothing I could say to her. She was babbling. Husbands lie to wives, wives to husbands, children to parents, everyone to everyone.

Someone called out from the kitchen. It was the old long-haired handyman—his name was Amos. He was saying something we couldn't hear. Jo shrugged and walked back into the kitchen. I followed.

Amos looked as pale as a ghost. His hands were clasped behind his neck as if he were about to try some exotic calisthenics.

"What's the matter with you, Amos?" Jo asked, half-angry, half-solicitous.

"I just came from down the road," Amos said, his voice scratchy and broken, "and they told me what happened. They murdered Mona Aspen last night, just like Mr. Starobin. They murdered her and hung her on a door."

6

All the heaters in the cottage were on, but it was very cold. What a bizarre way to spend New Year's Eve, I thought. I sat in the rocker, two blankets around me, like an old whaling woman in New Bedford waiting for the fleet to return. Bushy was lying on his back in front of one of the heaters. Pancho was cautiously circling the room, still confused because there were no high cabinets.

The small traveling clock beside the cot read 11:25. When, in fact, had been the last time I had a good New Year's Eve? It was a long time ago, when I had been in New York only about two years. I had gone to a party in the West Village, filled with young actors and actresses and designers and writers, all hungry, all dedicated, all expounding youthful theories. As I rocked, I pictured the apartment and the food and the drinks, but I couldn't remember a single name. Where were they all now?

A knock on the cottage door brought me out of my reverie. For a moment I was afraid. Then I heard Jo calling my name. She walked in carrying a bottle and several manila envelopes.

"I just couldn't be alone on New Year's Eve," she said, "and I found some old table wine."

I went into the small kitchen and brought back two glasses. The wine was terrible, but so what? Seeing Jo slump into the rocker, I sat on the cot.

"Last New Year's Eve, Harry and I consumed a whole bottle of pear brandy." She paused and rocked. "Well," she added, "maybe it was the year before." She laughed crazily, despairingly, and then: "But there won't be any pear brandy ever again . . . will there?"

Pancho began to circle the rocker. Jo put her glass on the rocker arm, then decided it was not secure and placed it on the floor. Pancho flew away.

"I thought," she said, tapping the manila envelopes she held on her lap, "that we should start looking through it all tonight."

She stood up, walked to the cot, placed the envelopes down on it, and returned to the rocker. I could see the writing on the top envelope: "1980–1981."

Her request startled me. It was New Year's Eve, almost midnight. She had brought in some wine, seeking company. It wasn't the right time to start digging through old letters.

I looked at her skeptically. She stared back

at me—defiant, a bit frightened, a bit pleading.

Suddenly I realized why she had brought the envelopes to me. If her neighbor—that woman Mona Aspen—had been murdered in the same manner as Harry, it might mean that the police were right. Perhaps a pack of homicidal house thieves was prowling the area, breaking into houses for valuables. Harry's murder might have been just a random event; he was in the wrong place at the wrong time. Jo didn't want to believe that.

I opened an envelope and shook a few items out onto the blanket. The first was a letter in a torn envelope. It was written to Harry from a woman in California who asked for advice in the raising of Russian blues. Her handwriting was very hard to read. I could see a mark on the upper-right-hand corner of the letter, signifying that Harry had answered it and noting the date he had answered it.

The next item was a request from a man in Madison, New Jersey, who wrote that he had met Harry at a cat show in Philadelphia and now he needed an out-of-print book on eye disease in cats. Did Harry know where he could get hold of a copy? Again there was the telltale mark on the corner indicating that Harry had responded—but there was no way to tell what his response had been. I started to look at the next item—a note attached to a newspaper clipping—when I heard Jo say: "Please, I didn't mean you should start right now. I thought . . . I mean, we must drink the wine, at least until midnight." I put the clipping down.

Jo started to rock furiously in her chair. She closed her eyes and said, "Mona Aspen was a wonderful woman. Did you know that."

"I didn't know her at all," I replied.

"I thought maybe you had been to see her horses and met her.

"Was she a breeder?"

"No. Mona's place is down the road. It's a layover barn. Trainers send their sick and broken-down racehorses to her. She nurses them back to health. Years ago there used to be many horse farms around here—layover barns, breeding barns, and all kinds of horses. Now, only Mona was left."

I looked at the clock. We had missed the moment. Happy New Year.

"Such a wonderful, kindly woman," Jo said, "and such a good friend to Harry and me."

"Her husband. Is her husband still alive?" I asked, remembering that the handyman had, during his disjointed conversation, once referred to her as Mrs. Aspen.

"I don't know. He lives in Connecticut, I think, or he did live there. They were divorced ages ago. Mona's nephew and his wife live on the farm with her."

"How old was Mona Aspen?" I asked.

"Oh, about five years younger than I. But much more vigorous. She still mucked out stalls."

"Did she keep valuables in the house?"

"No, I don't think so. Oh, wait—antiques, yes, a lot of old things like vases and writing desks and paintings and such. Mona was a great one for horse paintings. But I don't know if they were really worth anything."

She drifted off into a private reverie. I returned to the items on the blanket for a moment, and then lay back—I didn't feel like going through them anymore at that time. I was tired and cold. The wine was playing tricks in my nose.

"I must get back to the house now," Jo said a bit grimly. But she didn't move off the rocker.

Then she said, "Will you come to the cemetery tomorrow for Mona's funeral? There will be only a short graveyard ceremony."

I nodded. She got up, smiled in a motherly, almost beatific fashion, and left with the empty wine bottle.

I started to undress, then noticed that I had hung my winter coat on the hook behind the door. Just as the killers had hung Harry after they were through with him. The coat had to come down. If I woke during the night, as was my fashion, and saw it hanging in the darkness, there would be an ugly panic. I removed the coat from the hook and placed it on the back of the rocker.

What a strange little cemetery it was! The headstones were ancient, chipped, obscured.

The grounds lay behind a huge new shopping center just off the main east-west road. A strong, swirling wind whipped the overgrown weeds against the legs of the eight or ten mourners. A minister with a large muffler wrapped around his neck said the words over the open grave. Two men with shovels and one with a small earth mover stayed about twenty yards behind the mourners, waiting for the ceremony to conclude. One of them cupped a lighted cigarette in his hand.

Jo held on to my arm tightly. She said in a desperate whisper so close to my ear I could feel her lips, "I'm glad I did what Harry asked. No funeral. No burial. I cremated him and spread the ashes on the gravel driveway from the road to the house. I could not have survived him being buried in this place."

The thought struck me as grotesque. I shivered, realizing that every time I walked to the main house I would be crunching Harry deeper into oblivion.

As the minister began the final prayer, Jo continued to hold tight to me. She was beginning to restrict the circulation in my arm, but I didn't have the heart to pull away.

"God, Alice," she said, her voice breaking, "what a good friend she was to us . . . to me and to Harry and to Ginger. What a wonderful and kind woman she was."

It was over. We threw some dirt on the grave and started back to the car. A couple came up and began to speak to Jo. Feeling out of place, I walked to the car to wait for her.

A large man was leaning against the fender. It was Detective Senay. Another plainclothes detective sat in an unmarked car near the cemetery entrance.

"Cat-sitting again?" Senay asked.

"Something like that."

"Did you get that list from Mrs. Starobin?"

"What list?" I asked.

"The inventory of valuables."

"No."

"You know, Mrs. Aspen's nephew is cooperating with us. I don't understand why Starobin's widow isn't."

"Maybe, Detective, it's because there were no valuables in the house."

"What were they looking for? Chicken soup?"

I was about to tell him that Jo didn't believe Harry was murdered by random breaking-and-entering thieves. But I didn't. "Were the killings the same?" I asked.

"Close. Mona Aspen was murdered by a blunt instrument. We'll get them. They'll have to sell what they took. We'll get them. And we'll get them quicker if Mrs. Starobin helps."

"Ask her yourself. I'm not really working for the Nassau County Police Department," I noted.

"I have asked her, and I'll keep asking her.

By the way, who are you working for, Mrs. Nestleton?"

"I'm not married," I said.

"Too bad."

"Sez you."

"You know, I have a funny feeling about you," he said, taking off his hat and passing it from hand to hand.

"That's your problem, Detective."

He nodded, smiled, waved his hand, and walked toward the unmarked car.

Jo and I drove back to the house in silence. I made no mention of my brief strange conversation with Senay. As we approached the drive, Jo said: "Do you think that Mona's nephew will find in their deposit box what I found in my safe-deposit box?"

The logic of her question was so startling and so plausible that I almost laughed out loud in discomfort. Why not? I thought.

I didn't get a chance to answer. Jo laughed suddenly. Then she said, "How stupid of me! If Mona had that kind of cash she probably gave it to her nephew straight out to bail him out of his gambling debts. That young man was always in trouble, and poor Mona just kept cleaning up after him as best she could. He looks and talks like a gentleman, but believe me, he's not housebroken."

She laughed again, a quieter, almost wry laugh this time, then continued. "Harry used to say that we old Long Island families were like carefully piled stacks of kindling. Lovely on the outside but a world of maggots underneath."

She dropped me off where the path to the cottage begins. As I walked toward the cottage I saw the caretaker, Amos, staring at me, leaning against a short ladder right outside the garage. He didn't wave. He made me uncomfortable. I didn't like him and I think the dislike was reciprocated.

I went into the cottage and fed the cats. They were sulking, unhappy. "Get used to it, my friends," I said. "Momma has to make a living." Then I relented and promised Pancho some saffron rice when we got back to Manhattan.

I spent the next two hours attempting to straighten up the cramped cottage. As I did, I felt increasingly as if I had missed something important. I made a cup of tea and sat down on the rocker. Bushy leapt onto my lap to get scratched.

I knew it was something that Jo had said.

As the day progressed, that "something" began to fester in my head. I kept closing my eyes and reconstructing the conversations I had had during the past twenty-four hours. The clue was very close to consciousness but kept slipping away, like the name of an old friend or an old restaurant.

It finally caught up with me, as usual, after I had stopped worrying about it. I was doing the dishes in the tiny sink with one of the brillo pads that Jo had so kindly left me.

On New Year's Eve Jo had told me what a good friend Mona Aspen had been to herself and Harry. But at the cemetery Jo had told me what a wonderful friend Mona Aspen had been to herself and Harry *and* Ginger.

It could mean, of course, absolutely nothing. But it could mean an awful lot. Two people had been brutally murdered, and a stable girl was friend to one, lover to the other. I had to find out where Ginger had gone.

7

We were sitting at the kitchen table. In front of us was a carton marked "1985." Beside the carton were piles of paper and two empty coffee cups and a plate with uneaten toast. We had been working for about an hour and had developed a procedure in our search. One of us would pick up a letter or note or bill, study it, then briefly recite the contents to the other. If not suspicious, we went on to the next one.

Jo was wearing Harry's old volunteer fire-department jacket; it was always freezing in their house. "That detective stopped by early this morning when I was in the barn. It must have been seven o'clock. He keeps bothering me about that list." She paused in her recital and stared at one of her cats.

Then she continued, "I keep telling him that nothing was stolen that I know of. He doesn't believe me. I am beginning to dislike that man. He's devious. He also asked me if Mona and Harry were in business together. And then he asked about their relationship. I really did not like the way he used the word 'relationship,' as if they were in the Mafia."

I laughed. Harry in the Mafia was a funny image. But I wasn't really interested in Senay's inquiries. I was interested in Ginger.

"What did you mean yesterday, Jo, when you said that Mona Aspen and Ginger were good friends?"

"Well, they *were* good friends. Mona was the one who sent Ginger to us for a job."

"I'm confused, Jo. Was she living at Mona's?"

"That I don't remember. Maybe. But they were friends. Even when she was working for me, Ginger used to go over to Mona's to help her out in a pinch. If a horse was really sick, or when the blacksmith came."

"What is Ginger's last name?"

Jo sat back with a testy flourish of her hands. "I honestly don't remember. Why are you asking me all these questions about Ginger?"

I waited for a moment to let her calm down. "Where did she live when she was working for you?" I asked.

"I don't know. Not far from here. But a lot of the time she just slept in the barn."

"Jo," I said, very gently so it would not appear as a demand, although I was surely willing to make it a demand if Jo became difficult, "I want to talk to Ginger."

The request startled her. "Well, I don't know where she is."

"Who would know?"

"Maybe Nick."

"Who's Nick?"

"Nicholas Hill. Mona's nephew. You saw him at the cemetery."

"Can we go there now?"

Jo exploded. "But here is where Harry is," she yelled, plunging her hand into the pile of aging letters, bills, and notes.

"Calm down, Jo. Listen to me. I have the very uncomfortable feeling that the one person on earth who knew Harry and Mona best was the stable girl. Do you understand?"

Jo shook her head, keeping her face averted from me. "What a cruel thing to say," she replied.

It was cruel. But I had no option. I was making a point.

Suddenly Jo's face lit up and she said, "Wait, I remember her last name. It was Mauch. Ginger Mauch." Then she said wearily, "Okay. Let's drive over to see Nick. I don't want to fight with you, Alice. We need each other."

It was a two-minute drive from the broken-down Starobin farm to the freshly painted, well-manicured complex of buildings over which Mona Aspen had once presided. I followed Jo across a fenced field to the stable area. Nicholas Hill was just inside one of the barns, laboriously cleaning a shovel. I could see the heads of the racehorses as we entered. They were peering out of their stalls without much concern. A few were grabbing chunks of hay from hay nets hung outside their stalls.

Nicholas was a middle-aged graying man, well-dressed even when working. He nodded to us, but kept on cleaning the shovel.

I remembered that Jo had said he was a heavy gambler. He didn't look like a man who would take large bills out of his pocket and bet them on a horse. But then again, I didn't look like a woman who did cat-sitting. Nicholas banged the shovel on the ground to shake more dirt loose. His hands were large, lined, and powerful.

A slouch hat with a fishing feather tucked into it was precariously perched on his head. It was an odd hat for winter.

"We're trying to find Ginger," Jo said almost happily.

Nick let the shovel drop and stared at it reflectively. He seemed to think he was not doing a good job. Then he looked up, smiling at Jo, removed a glove, and blew on the hand. His actions were very measured, calm.

"I haven't seen her since about a week before she left your place," he finally replied.

"Do you know where she lives?" I butted in.

He smiled at Jo again as if they both understood it was a stupid question but one that could be expected from an outsider.

"I never knew," he replied. "although she did stay with us for a while some time ago. But so what? She was just another wounded thing my aunt picked up. That was Mona, wasn't it? Wounded birds. Wounded people. 'Get out of the car, Nicholas,' she used to say, 'and see if that smashed squirrel is still alive.' Of course, he had been dead for a week."

I could tell by his tone—alternately bitter and loving—that it would be a long time before he would get over the death of his aunt.

"Anyway," he continued, still looking at Jo, "when Ginger started to work for the Starobins, she got her own place. No, wait. It was before that. I remember she kept moving around from place to place, because she was always borrowing my pickup truck. Look, I never said more than ten words to that girl!"

What a strange thing for him to say. Why should he make such a comment? It was as if speaking to Ginger would implicate him in something. What was he afraid of? I didn't trust Mona's nephew one bit. A horse whinnied in a stall down the aisle, and then came two, three, four explosive sounds, like gunshots. Frightened, I stepped back, toward the entrance to the barn.

"Relax," Nicholas said, "that's only the new filly they shipped in from Philadelphia Park. Eye infection—nothing serious, but she's crazy as a loon. She just loves kicking walls."

A gust of wind blew down the center of the aisle, stinging our eyes and ears. Nick tried to pull his hat down on his head. "There's coffee in the house, Jo," he said.

As Jo shook her head, I asked, "Would you have any idea where Ginger is now?"

"Well, she used to be friendly with a guy

named Bobby Lopez. He works in the Chevron station on Route 106. Do you know it?"

Jo nodded that she did, smiled at Nick, and we both started walking back toward the car.

We hadn't gone more than twenty feet when Nick called, "Jo!" We looked back. He was leaning on the shovel, his face now a bright red from the wind. "Jo, do you think we'll survive the winter?"

Jo stared at him dumbly for a moment, then walked quickly back to him. I saw them embrace. I heard sobs. I turned away. I didn't want to intrude in their shared sorrow—but I felt a longing to be with them, to hold and be held. It was silly. What really had Mona and Harry been to me? Or I to them? And yet these two murdered people were beginning to envelop me in a peculiar way, as if there had always been another me—another Alice Nestleton longing to be part of them. The whole thing was perplexing.

Minutes later, we found Bobby Lopez sipping coffee in one of the repair bays of the Chevron station. At his feet was an enormous mongrel bitch with floppy ears who kept rolling over and over.

Bobby had a beautiful face with deep-set almond eyes. He didn't appear happy to see us at all. His hands and arms were stained with a bluish grease. But he answered our questions with dispatch. Yes, he said, he knew Ginger. No, he said, he hadn't seen her in weeks. Yes, he said, he knew where she lived.

When we asked where specifically, he balked for the first time. "Why do you want to know?" he asked suspiciously.

Jo was wonderful. She lied like a producer. She told Bobby Lopez that Ginger was still owed a week's wages and she wanted to deliver the money to her.

He smiled grimly at us and lit a cigarette. He prodded the dog playfully. He stared at Jo, then at me. He seemed to be evaluating us against some standard.

Finally he said, "She lives over the Tarpon Bar in Oyster Bay Village. It's right at the crossroads of the town. You can't miss it unless you want to."

His knowledge of her lodgings sort of dripped with the idea that they were both very close—lovers, in fact. Jo asked, "Where did you meet her?" And her voice was so incredulous that the mechanic bristled. He understood what she meant. How could a nice girl like Ginger end up with a grease monkey? Jo was making her class prejudice explicit.

"At Aqueduct racetrack, lady. We both used to work for Charlie Coombs."

Bobby Lopez was right. One couldn't miss the Tarpon Bar if one drove through the center of Oyster Bay Village. In a hallway next to the bar, we found Ginger Mauch's name on a mailbox.

A very rickety staircase took us up. The landings needed paint. The floors were covered with pocked linoleum. The doors of the apartments were warped.

Ginger Mauch lived on the third floor in the rear apartment. The door was wide open. A few pieces of furniture were scattered throughout the single large room. The closet was open and empty. The drawers of the dresser were open and empty.

Ginger had obviously moved out in haste.

In one corner of the large room, in front of the window, was a pile of posters, clothes, records, and other items she had obviously discarded as not important enough to take with her. I could see some unopened cans of soup in the pile.

"Poor Ginger," Jo said, sitting down wearily on a folding chair.

I was mystified. Why had she moved out in such a rush? Was she frightened? Of what? The more I tried to comprehend the stable girl and her behavior, the more elusive she became.

Jo stood up suddenly and walked toward the pile of discarded junk.

"Do you see anything, Jo?" I asked, because her move was purposeful.

Her foot had found something and was pulling it out from the pile, like it was something dirty. It was a photograph of a laughing Harry standing in front of the barn, a calico cat draped around his neck like a muffler. He was smiling his wonderful smile.

"My God," Jo whispered, "I've been looking

for this photograph for a year. It's the best photo Harry ever took. And that's Veronica, the barn cat, on him. Harry told me the picture had just vanished, but he was lying. He gave it to Ginger. Why would he do that? And now she just left it in a pile of garbage."

Her foot pushed the photo back into the pile. The corners were discolored.

I bent over to pick it up.

"Leave it, please leave it," she said, sitting back down on the flimsy folding chair, the color drained from her face.

I left it alone, and instead looked about the room. My gaze settled on the denuded wire hangers in the closet. The more elusive Ginger became, the more I realized I had to find her.

"Do you know Charlie Coombs?" I asked Jo, remembering what Bobby Lopez had said.

"The trainer?"

"Is he a trainer? I'm talking about the name Bobby Lopez mentioned."

"Yes. Of course he's a trainer. I know him. He used to lay up horses at Mona's place. Just like his father did before him. A lot of trainers swore by Mona. She had a healing touch with sick horses, like Harry did with all animals. Old Man Coombs even used to call Mona when he had problems training a yearling . . ."

She paused, then added in a choked voice, "It seems like all the wonderful people are gone."

I walked over to Jo and took her hand,

squeezing it. "Come with me back to Manhattan, Jo, for a day or two. We'll go to Aqueduct. Charlie Coombs may know where Ginger is. If she worked for him before, maybe she went back to him."

"I'm very tired, Alice," she said.

"But Harry and Mona are dead, Jo, and we won't find their killers in this pile of junk or in Harry's pile of junk in the storeroom."

Jo stared at me for a moment, then at our joined hands. "Okay, Alice. Why not? What else are old ladies for?"

8

I was sitting in my apartment watching Jo prowl. My apartment fascinated her. She kept walking from one end to the other, picking up things, putting them down. I didn't understand her acute interest, particularly after a long day. Was it conceivable that a wise old woman like Jo thought the life of an actress to be exciting and glamorous, reflected somehow in her furniture and bric-a-brac? There was not one glamorous item in my apartment.

Finally she sat down on the sofa and said, "Well, I hope all the cats survive. The last time I left them with Amos, I was afraid he was going to eat them." She stared down at Bushy as if contemplating Amos contemplating eating him.

It was nine o'clock in the evening. We were both very tired, and Jo had said we had to leave at five-thirty the following morning because trainers exercise their horses really early. If we wanted to speak to Charlie Coombs, we had to catch him then.

"Do you want some tea, Jo, or something stronger?"

"Nothing, thank you," she said, looking around again with that wide-eyed curiosity. Then she smiled. "You know, Alice, I just never thought your apartment would look like this."

"Like what, Jo?"

"Well . . . so . . . so conservative."

"Did you think I led a wild life in the big city, Jo?"

"I didn't know what to think."

"Men are scarce, Jo, at least at this time."

"But you're a beautiful woman," she blurted. I didn't know how to respond. Maybe she wanted me to recount my brief fling at promiscuity. But that had happened a long time ago, after my marriage had broken up, and I remembered little about it. Furthermore, it was none of her business.

When I looked at her again, she was crying. I closed my eyes and opened them again only when she began to speak: "You want to hear something funny, Alice? I was a virgin when I married Harry. And I never slept with another man. Only Harry. So if I die tomorrow or the day after, I'll never really know if what Harry and I had was real love . . . or real passion. Do you know what I mean, Alice?"

"It's not too late," I quipped, and then was immediately chagrined at the stupidity of my remark.

She smiled at me. "Oh, I think it is. I think it is."

Bushy was now circling the sofa, wondering

whether to jump up on the strange woman who had captured his favorite place. He looked alternately confused and angry. His tail switched. His ears did what passes for a Maine coon cat's dance.

I went to the hall closet and pulled out pillows, a quilt, and a woolen blanket older than me that had been on my grandmother's farm in Minnesota. It was a strange blue—like a frayed psychotic sky. I laid all the bedding on a chair next to the sofa, along with a clean towel for Jo. Then I went to sleep.

When we pulled up at the racetrack entrance the next morning, we found it manned by uniformed guards who were very suspicious. For some reason, I had always thought the racetrack was open, like a mall. I soon found out otherwise, for they would not let us in. First of all, Jo couldn't get Charlie Coombs on the phone. He was somewhere on the racetrack but not available. Then, when she finally contacted him, we had to wait for passes to be made out. And then, after we were through the gate, we got hopelessly lost in the barn areas. "I haven't been here in twenty years," Jo kept telling me by way of explanation.

It was past six-thirty when we reached Charlie Coombs's stalls. Suddenly we were surrounded by horses that had just come back from their morning workouts. They were steaming from sweat in the freezing morning.

Young men and women stripped their saddles and bridles, covered them with blankets, and then started to walk them in slow circles around the stable area, guiding them with rope halters.

I had never been that close to racehorses before, and was staggered by their power. I could sense that they were only a step away from flight. These majestic beasts were capable of bursts of awesome speed. And even in the darkness I could sense their individuality—an eye, a turn of the head, a sudden distinctive whinny. Of course they frightened me, but I longed to make some kind of contact with all that power.

Jo pulled me out of an almost trancelike state, and together we entered a small cluttered office. Seated behind his desk, Charlie Coombs was talking on the phone when he saw us, and he gestured emphatically with his hand that we should sit and wait.

People came in and out of the office without saying a word, wearing riding helmets or stocking caps, bundled up against the cold, their movements quick, almost choppy, as they used the coffee machine occupying the only uncluttered spot in the office. Next to the machine were containers of sugar and milk and a large cardboard box on which was crudely written: "If you drink coffee, pay for the coffee." I saw no one drop any money into the box.

Finally Charlie Coombs slammed the phone

down and said, "Jo, I heard about Harry and Mona Aspen. God, I'm sorry." He raised both palms as if emphasizing that the world is like that—full of unexplained misery and loss.

I liked the man immediately. He looked around forty-five or fifty, with a weather-beaten, aggressive face but a very kindly smile. He had thick graying black hair which went every which way, and he was dramatically underdressed considering the cold—a dress shirt without a tie, and over it a kind of hunter's vest.

Jo introduced us to each other. He leaned forward and said, "I like Jo's friends . . . under any circumstances."

I could see that he was shorter than I thought—and he was wearing red sneakers. For some reason, that made me feel very good. Imagine a man training million-dollar race-horses with red sneakers. It was poetic and crazy, a kind of equine *Red Shoes*, only Charlie Coombs was obviously no Moira Shearer. He was trying to give us his full attention, but it was obvious that one part of him was outside the office, focused on the horses, listening for trouble signs or whatever trainers listen for.

Jo said, "We're trying to locate Ginger Mauch."

"But, Jo, she works for you," he replied.

"She quit. Suddenly. She just went and quit."

"Well, I don't know where she is, then. Jo, I haven't seen Ginger in a couple of years."

"But she used to work for you," I said, realizing it was time for me to start leading the conversation.

"Right. She worked here for about six months. Then she quit. Then I heard she was helping out Mona Aspen on the Island. Then I heard she was working for Harry and Jo."

"Do you remember the circumstances under which you hired her?" I asked him.

My rather pretentious question made Coombs laugh. He leaned over toward me—a bit threatening, a bit flirtatious. "Before I answer that question, I want to know what business you're in."

"Why?"

"Well, it's the kind of question an IRS agent would ask."

"I'm an actress."

He stepped back, looking at me intently; it was obviously not what he had expected to hear.

Jo intervened apologetically. "Charlie, we just need all the information you can give us about Ginger. We don't have time to explain."

"The circumstances," Coombs said, skillfully mimicking my pretentious language, "were, if I remember—she came into my office and asked me for a job as an exercise rider. I told her I didn't need exercise riders, but I did need an assistant trainer to do all the paperwork I couldn't do . . . and a lot of other stupid tasks around the barn, from ordering hay to dealing with security. I told her that since I had become rich and famous I needed more time for myself. She said okay. I hired her."

"Did she tell you anything about herself?"

"Not really. I did learn eventually that she was born and raised in Vermont, that she usually came to work late on Thursday for some reason, and that she took milk and no sugar in her coffee."

I could see that he was making an honest effort to remember. "Did you ask her for references?"

"No. I didn't have to. Ginger was an exercise rider in Maryland before she came to New York. And the horse she rode was Cup of Tea. She showed me clippings."

"Cup of Tea!" Jo repeated in a startled voice. "She never told me about that."

"Who is Cup of Tea?" I asked, bewildered by Jo's response.

Charlie Coombs walked back behind the desk and sat down. He grinned wickedly at me in a good-natured way, as if I should be ashamed of myself. "Once upon a time," he began in a self-mocking pedagogic tone, "there was an ugly little foal born on a farm in upper Michigan. He was a thoroughbred, but from a very undistinguished family. Nobody ever heard of his momma or papa. They called him Cup of Tea because his color was so murky—not bay, not chestnut. He actually looked like a cow pony, which is why he was auctioned off as a yearling for only nine hundred dollars.

"The new owner took Cup of Tea around the Midwest circuit—racing him in the cheapest races at the cheapest dirt tracks. He always lost. So he was sold to a trainer in Maryland, who wanted to make him into a track pony. Well, Cup of Tea goes to Maryland and starts accompanying real racehorses out onto the track to keep them calm.

"One day the little horse accompanies a hotshot allowance horse out onto the track for a grass workout. Cup of Tea, who probably never saw a grass track in his life, spooked, threw his rider, and ran around the grass track about two seconds faster than the world record for that distance.

"To make a long story short, the next year Cup of Tea wins the three biggest grass stakes in America, including the Budweiser Million. And right now the old boy is the most expensive and sought after stud in the world, standing in France. It's the ultimate rags-to-riches story. It's Hollywood."

It was a wonderful story. I could see it as a movie. But who would play Ginger?

A young Hispanic man burst into the office and yelled something in Spanish to Coombs. The trainer nodded, stood up, and said, "I hope I was of some help."

He shook Jo's hand and kissed her lightly on top of her head. Then he said to me, "I like telling you horse stories. I have plenty of them. I even have some other kinds of stories."

I leaned over the desk and wrote my number on his pad.

"His father was even nicer," Jo said after he left.

I mulled over this new information on Ginger as we drove back to Manhattan and double-parked until it was time for the alternate-side-of-the-street parking clock to change. From what I could tell, we were no closer to learning her present whereabouts than we had been before.

"What do we do now?" Jo asked.

"Wait until we can park legally and then eat. There's a Chinese restaurant right up the block, with good lunch specials."

"I mean about Ginger."

"We keep looking."

"But who else can we contact? Who else knows her?"

"That horse."

Jo laughed. "Isn't it a wonderful story? Cup of Tea is a lovable horse."

A car drove by too fast, flinging slush against our windows. Finally we were able to park. When we entered the restaurant, I realized the old woman was tired. She stared at the menu as if in a daze and then ordered exactly what I ordered.

She ate the sizzling rice soup but left the rest of her meal. I ate everything. I was hungry and cold. And I was still excited by the racetrack, by the proximity of the horses . . . and by Charlie Coombs.

"I'm just not hungry," Jo said by way of apology, appalled by the realization that she was wasting food.

When we paid the bill and stepped outside, we found that a brilliant winter sun had broken through the clouds. Everything was brighter, warmer, cleaner.

"I'm tired," Jo said. "I could use a nap."

"It's only two minutes to my apartment," I assured her.

As I looked down the street, mentally rechecking where we had parked the car, I noticed a small red pickup truck had already double-parked in front of it. Good, I thought, it would protect the windows from slush.

I looked at Jo. She was standing contentedly, her face up to the sun.

The red pickup truck in front of her car started to move. I watched it casually, the sun sparkling along its red sides. Something was wrong, though. The truck crossed to the far side of the street, where no cars were parked— the illegal side.

It began to accelerate, and one set of wheels squealed against the curb. The little red truck was coming straight at us.

I grabbed Jo's arm. I started to run, pulling Jo with me.

I heard a screaming, grinding noise behind

me. Terrified, I tried to run faster. My legs started to wobble like jelly.

I heard a person scream. Showers of glass rained down. All went dark.

9

"Only one more landing to go," I said to Jo as we both hovered on the cusp between the third and fourth landings, exhausted, still dazed. Jo had a large bandage on one side of her face. I had a dressing across the top of my forehead right at the scalp line.

Noticing that one of the tenants still had a Christmas wreath on the door, I snarled. Why hadn't it been removed? Christmas was over and done with. And as I stood there between landings, holding Jo, I remembered some lines from a play I had once appeared in. A woman faces a hated husband and says, "What I'd like on this ominous Christmas Eve is a visitation from Baby Jesus, or at least a Christ in some highly recognizable form."

What was the name of the play? The playwright? The character? I could remember nothing, only those lines.

I touched my thigh gingerly. It hurt very badly. The doctors in the emergency room at Beekman Downtown Hospital had said nothing was broken, just bruised.

The police had told us the truck had crashed

into a lightpost, destroyed a parking sign, smashed the windows of the Chinese restaurant, destroyed a hydrant, spun around twice—and driven off. They told us we were very lucky. Drunk drivers like that one usually ended up killing or maiming people—and both of us had been only inches from death. It was a miracle, they said, that we had escaped with only superficial wounds from the flying glass.

We started up the final flight to my apartment, Jo in front, my hand lightly on her back to make sure she didn't fall. Or perhaps my staying behind her was not altruistic. When I had gained consciousness I had seen one side of her face drenched in blood from dozens of tiny glass cuts. And her cropped white hair had been flecked with blood. The sight had made me ill.

Finally, sanctuary. We both dropped onto the sofa like stones. We didn't move. We didn't speak.

It was already dark outside and there were no lights in the apartment. I realized I should turn on a light, but for the moment I couldn't intellectually locate the switch.

When I finally did turn it on and returned to the sofa, I saw Bushy and Pancho sitting calmly, side by side, staring at us. It was a very unusual pose for Pancho. He seemed to be assessing the situation. It must be our bandages, I thought. The white bandages must fascinate him.

"Can I get you something, Jo?"

"Nothing."

I stared at Pancho. I longed to cuddle with that crazy cat. For a brief moment I contemplated making a grab for him. But I didn't. Pancho was always too swift for me. He simply didn't want to cuddle. I smiled at him. His body was less relaxed. His curiosity was almost satiated. He would get back to business shortly—flight from the enemy.

Jo laughed, and I looked at her. Her hand was feeling her bandaged face. "I was just thinking," she explained, "how ridiculous it is to come into Manhattan and almost get killed by a drunk driver. I thought all the drunk drivers were on the Long Island Expressway."

"How do you know he was drunk, Jo?"

"Well, the police said he was drunk."

"Yes, they did."

"You have to be drunk to climb a curb and run your truck into a restaurant window."

We were both alive. It was time to deal with the facts. "He wasn't drunk, Jo. He was trying to kill us."

She barked a small, nervous laugh. "Alice, how do you know that?"

How did I know that? I closed my eyes and recreated the moments before. The driver of the red pickup truck had been idling his vehicle when we came out of the restaurant. He had crossed over from his double-parked position to the empty side to gather speed and then made a straight run toward us. I had seen him. I had known he was coming for us.

"He was trying to kill us, Jo."

"Why would anyone want to kill us?" she asked, skeptical, confused, disturbed.

I didn't answer her question. I looked at the cats. Pancho was gone. Bushy was stretched out. My thigh was throbbing like there was a frog under the skin.

The little red pickup truck had splintered all my idealistic pretensions. It had made me realize that my life was still precious to me. Sure, I had not become a great actress doing great roles, but there was still my craft, and my cats, and my apartment, and the hundreds of tiny things that constitute a life . . . and which I loved very much.

The red pickup truck had put the question forthrightly: Was I prepared to sacrifice it all to find out who murdered Harry Starobin?

No, I was not.

"Jo," I said as gently as possible, "they tried to murder us because we wouldn't let your husband rest in peace."

"I don't believe that, Alice. I have a right to find out who murdered Harry."

It was such a naive and ludicrous statement that I reacted sharply. "Don't be stupid, Jo. I'm not talking about rights. I'm talking about all that cash in your vault and God-knows-what elsewhere. I'm talking about people who murder other people. Do you want to die, Jo?

Those people, whoever they are, tried to kill us. And they'll try again if we don't stop."

She didn't respond. She leaned her head back against the sofa pillows. A tiny speck of blood was seeping out of her bandage.

I knew what she was thinking, that her good friend Alice was abandoning Harry. Yes, I was doing that. I was abandoning Harry and saving my life and hers. We had both gotten in too deep. We had both scratched the surface of something that was very dangerous.

"So you just want us to stop," she said, "to leave it all to that terrible Detective Senay who doesn't know a thing about Harry . . . who doesn't care about Harry."

"Yes."

"I should just go home and forget all about Harry's papers and his death and that money, and all about Mona. Is that what I should do?"

"Just proceed with your life, Jo."

"What life?"

"Any life you can make."

"It's easy for you to say, Alice."

She started to get up, but the effort was too much.

"Please don't be mad at me, Jo, please."

She flailed her arms in the air and then brought them to her lap. "I'm not mad at you, Alice. I'm . . . it's just that . . . poor Harry." And she began to mumble incoherently.

I covered her with a blanket and sat close to her. She had, I knew, accepted my decision, and I was relieved. I knew she was not capable of carrying on an investigation alone. We would both be safe if we distanced ourselves from Harry's corpse . . . or rather his gravel-strewn ashes. But along with the relief came no small amount of shame. I had, after all, quit. The role was too difficult for me. The consequences were too potentially dangerous. I was too old for a fling like that. Pancho flew by along the far wall, heading toward the windowsills. I was safe. We were all safe.

10

It was the first day of February, a brooding, frigid day. I had just returned from a lunch meeting with my agent and "some people." As usual, this kind of meeting had agitated me. I was not well-known enough as an actress to be offered parts like pieces of fruit, but I was too experienced and well-thought-of to be asked to read for many parts that I would have been delighted to read for. So, hoisted on that peculiar contradiction, I was always forced to have those strange, frustrating lunches with "some people" who were about to do a play or a movie or a PBS special.

The whole thing was a sham anyway, because I hadn't done any straight theater for a long time. I wasn't interested in that stuff anymore. I was looking for parts that stretched the imagination, that took reality apart, and one didn't find them with "some people." I never left a lunch with them without muttering, "god bless cat-sitting."

So there I was, sitting on the sofa, indulging my latest bad habit—touching the small crescent-shaped scar which remained on the top of my forehead after they removed the bandage.

A variant of my usual theatrical fantasy was beginning to form. I was appearing as a guest artist in some exotic foreign company—like the Moscow Arts Theater. My role was minor, but as the play unfolded, I spoke my lines and exhibited such awesome stage presence that my character totally overwhelmed the major characters in the play. At the end, roses were flung at me—large blood-red roses—as if I were a ballerina. It was such an egotistical adolescent fantasy that it always embarrassed me—but it never went away. And the fantasy always afforded me, during its course, intense joy, and why not?

It was a magical, mystical, lunatic fantasy, and in each reenactment the vehicle changed. It was a Victorian costume drama. It was a sleazy detective drama. It was a Brechtian interpretation of the Theban Cycle.

"Oh, Bushy," I said, "how stupid and weary I am . . . and how bizarre my whole life has become—lunches and fantasies and kitty litter." Bushy understood. That is what cats are all about.

The phone rang. I figured it was my agent calling to tell me how the lunch had gone, how those "people" were excited by my talents. I let the phone ring a long time because I really didn't want to talk to her. She was a nice foolish woman but she had begun to harp on my stopping all that avant-garde nonsense and going back to where I "belonged"—Eugene O'Neill? And I kept saying, "Sure, get me some skinny Colleen Dewhurst parts." Both of us were lying.

When it didn't stop ringing, I picked it up. It wasn't my agent. It was Charlie Coombs, the trainer.

He said he had something even better than horse stories to tell me. He said that an exercise rider who works for him lives in my neighborhood and will drive me out to the track in the morning to see how a great—chuckle—trainer like himself really trains racehorses.

I stared at the phone. For the past few weeks I had thought about Charlie Coombs many times, but only in relation to Jo and her troubles, and I had not heard from Jo since she returned to Long Island, disgruntled at my defection.

But the moment I heard his voice on the phone, I knew that we would become lovers.

I don't really know why I thought that. The theater is no place for love. Actresses can't stand actors, and vice versa. The only men I met who weren't actors or directors were bankers and lawyers and businessmen on the fringes of the theater. They were perpetually fascinated by and panting for actresses who they thought would provide a new world of erotic and intellectual excitement. It never happened that way. The magic never emerged. I was by now more or less resigned to celibacy.

But how would it be with a man who had nothing to do with the theater?

I said I would be delighted to go out to the racetrack again.

"Malacca," he said, which was the name of the exercise rider, "will be in front of your house at four-thirty tomorrow morning." Then he hung up.

I turned to Bushy, who had just jumped up for some attention, and was just about to tell him about the Charlie Coombs phone call when the phone started ringing again. This time it had to be my agent. This time I had to let it ring. Or put the damn machine on, which I hated.

But what if it was Charlie with a change of plans?

I picked up the phone. It was Carla Fried.

"Alice, I'm at La Guardia. I have to catch a plane at Newark in three hours. If I go through Manhattan, we can meet for coffee."

"Where does the bus bring you?" I asked automatically, flustered by her call.

"I take it to Forty-second and Park. We can meet in the bar of the Grand Hyatt, across the street. An hour okay?"

"Fine," I said. And she hung up. God, that woman had become efficient. It was like dealing with a corporate jet.

Remembering that the bar of the Grand Hyatt was pseudo-posh, I threw on something pseudo-respectable.

Carla was waiting for me at the entrance to the bar inside the hotel lobby. She had taken a cab. The moment we sat down, she started to talk a mile a minute. She was sorry she hadn't called back after she left Atlanta. Everything about the production was going well. She wasn't going to pressure me about a decision on the part—there was still plenty of time. Then she sat back and grinned.

"I'm babbling, Alice, I'm sorry. Planes make me crazy."

We ordered drinks.

"What is going on with you?" she asked.

Her question seemed so absurd I started to laugh and then to cry. How could I tell her what had happened? How could I tell her about the murders? She wouldn't comprehend or care. How could I tell her about the fear when that little red truck came toward Jo and me?

"What's the matter, Alice? Are you sick?"

Her face clouded over with such concern that I felt terrible at spoiling our meeting.

"No, no, a man," I said quickly, recovering.

"A man? I had forgotten all about them," she quipped. "You mean those people with the funny musculature."

"I think I'm going to have an affair, Carla. And I'm a little nervous. It's been a long, long time."

"Who is he?"

"A man I met at the racetrack. A trainer."

"It has been so long since I had an affair, Alice, that when I go out for drinks with Waring—"

"Waring?" I interrupted, not remembering the name.

"The millionaire I told you about . . . the one who funded our season."

"I'm sorry. Of course I remember. Are you sleeping with him?"

"No. That's my point. He's smart and handsome and crazy and rich. The kind of man I always dreamed of. But now I just sit and talk theater with him, and not a single erotic thought pops out. You'll see. He's in New York. I called him from the airport after I talked to you. He'll be here to have a drink with us. But I want to hear about your man."

"Well, Charlie Coombs is not rich or handsome, but he may well be crazy."

"You can't have everything," she said.

Another round of drinks came and we lapsed into one of those wonderful, surreal, lewd, revealing conversations that are basically sexual autobiographies. It was delicious. We laughed. We cried. We remembered.

Suddenly I felt a touch on my shoulder. And then I heard a voice.

"So you're Juliet's Nurse," the voice said. I turned and stared at a man.

"I'm Waring," he said, and pulled a chair to our table, sitting easily.

Is he the pope? I thought sarcastically. Only

one name—Waring. Maybe all very rich men use only their last names—even in bed. He was tall and skinny. His thinning light hair was brushed back and longish. He was wearing an old brown corduroy suit with a beautiful light blue knit tie on a dark blue shirt. He looked like an academic. His face was lined, with blue eyes. Fifty? Sixty? I couldn't tell.

"Don't worry, I'm not going to harass you about the part," he said, "because Carla has been giving me all kinds of etiquette lessons about dealing with actresses."

His voice had that funny Canadian accent, a flattish inflection which is so difficult to describe and even harder to mimic.

He sat back and beamed at Carla. My curiosity immediately turned to hate. He was looking at Carla as if she were his possession. As if her theater group were his new toy. As if, just as he owned factories and wheat fields and oil tankers and racing cars and yachts and horses and dogs, now he was going to own a little theater and he was going to apply his magic touch and—poof—out would come another Moscow Arts Theater. God, he sickened me. He reminded me of a hundred other theatrical backers I had met over the years, people who shared his arrogance even though they had only one-millionth of Waring's fortune.

"What's the matter, Alice? You're pale. Are you sick?" Carla leaned toward me, her voice and face anxious.

I lied.

"No, I'm fine. It's just I forgot about an appointment . . . an important appointment. Look, I have to go. Call me! I'm still thinking about the part."

Then I stood up and walked out of there.

Malacca was waiting for me the next morning in a beat-up van, the back of which was filled with horse equipment, most of which I couldn't identify. He was a small man, obviously an ex-jockey, and he drove like a lunatic, sailing through lights happily, telling me his life story in violent bursts of energy, then falling silent, then erupting again.

When we reached Charlie Coombs's barn, the trainer was waiting for me. He smiled, and before I could say a word, he placed a riding hat on my head and buttoned the strap under my chin as if I were a total child. Then, taking me by the hand, he led me toward the saddled ponies standing quietly.

"This is Rose," he said, pointing to the larger one.

I hadn't been on a horse in fifteen years, but Rose was so gentle that it was like sitting on a pillow. Coombs climbed on the other pony and we started to pace forward. I needed a few moments to orient myself, since everything had happened so quickly, but I finally realized that all around us were racehorses, his racehorses, heading out to the track for their workouts.

As we continued to move en masse, I became unnerved. The horses were prancing, snorting, moving in often erratic patterns. Several of them looked crazed, as if they were about to bolt or rear up, and I heard the constant chatter of the exercise riders soothing them in Spanish. From time to time one of the racehorses would come close to my pony, Rose, and make contact with her. Rose was unperturbed. I was tense.

It was still dark, but there were tiny slivers of light beginning to infiltrate the horizon. Charlie brought his pony close to mine. "Okay?" he said. I nodded. He smiled. "Rose likes you," he said. He was projecting.

When we reached the gap in the track, the racehorses went out in single file. As each one passed Charlie, he gave the rider instructions—gallop such and such a distance, work the horse in such and such a time. Our two ponies drifted away from the gap and settled behind the rail.

"How do the riders know how fast they're going?" I asked, perplexed by the speeds Charlie had requested. They didn't carry stopwatches, and even if they did, they couldn't read them in the darkness.

"The clocks are in their heads," he replied.

Horses were now circling the track at different speeds. I couldn't identify Charlie's horses, but I saw from the way he was watching that he knew exactly where all of his horses were and what they were doing. Then

I too began to watch carefully. The sound of the hooves pounding the track was like a beautifully precise percussion instrument. I could see white froth on the horses' mouths. I intuited the strength and skill of the riders as they perched on top of their mounts so precarious, so light. The whole scene was packed with a kind of beauty, a kind of energy. Leaning all the way forward in the saddle and laying my head on Rose's shoulders, I closed my eyes and listened to the beat.

It was all over much too quickly. We rode back to the barn and Charlie took me through the barn area and into the stalls. He showed me how the horses were stripped and cooled off and then bedded down. He introduced me to the grooms and the riders and the barn cats and dogs who roamed freely in and out of the stalls. He showed me the horses that had not worked out that morning, allowing me to give them apples or pieces of sugar. He pointed out the feed problems and health problems. And then he led me back to his cluttered office, gave me some coffee and a piece of Danish pastry, and told me to wait until he finished up.

An hour later he was back, the morning work done. Now he looked exactly as I remembered him—underdressed, broad-shouldered, tousled hair, friendly manner.

But he was wearing boots.

"Where are your red sneakers?" I asked playfully.

"I don't wear them when I'm really trying to impress someone," he said.

"Well, to be honest, I found them very attractive."

"Damn," he said in mock anger, "I always make the wrong move." He sipped his coffee. Then he noted, "Jo sends her regards."

"You saw her?"

"No, I spoke to her. I called her and asked permission to call you."

"My God," I laughed, "that is old-fashioned."

"I am old-fashioned in most ways. Anyway, Jo told me you're no longer looking for Ginger Mauch."

"That's right. We gave it up." I noticed the way he looked at me, was really listening to me. I was flattered and my hand rose unconsciously to pat my hair.

"Jo told me you were both almost killed by a drunken driver."

"It was close. Very close."

"I see the scar," Coombs said, pointing to my forehead. I touched it once and pulled my hand away. I played with the uneaten Danish. I felt good sitting there. He made me feel very comfortable. His maturity was leavened with a kind of childishness. Maybe it came from working with horses.

He leaned over the desk a bit toward me. "By the way, are you a famous actress?"

"Not really. I'm more famous as a cat-sitter."

"I mean, should I know who you are? Should I have seen you in something?"

"If you were in Chapel Hill, North Carolina, in April 1985, you would have seen me do a very respectable Hedda Gabler. I'm not respectable anymore."

"My father used to tell me," Coombs said wryly, "that one has to be respectable to make it in the world. But what do fathers know?"

"What *do* fathers know?"

He didn't answer my absurd question, but instead looked mournful for a moment. He snapped out of it quickly, though, and laughed. "Do you want me to tell you more horse stories?"

I leaned back. "Tell me whatever you want to tell me," I replied. We were flirting with each other now, I realized. I didn't want to do that. What did I want to do?

He started to play with his coffee cup. "I shouldn't have asked you to come out here on such short notice," he apologized.

"Actually I like short notices. It seems as if a crisis exists—but there is none. One gets excitement and relief at the same time."

"There was a crisis," he said.

"What?"

"You. I wanted to see you."

"Well, you've seen me."

"Yes, the crisis is over. But I was always good at crises. Actually, that's why I'm a trainer. The racetrack is about crises. Something bad is always happening. A horse throws a rider. A cinch breaks. A dog bites a horse. A horse bites a vet. A trainer makes the wrong claim. I was always good in crises.''

"Is that why you don't wear enough clothes in winter?" I asked.

"Right. Stay light. Stay mobile," he replied, laughing, his rough face crinkling into an incredibly kindly smile.

"Do you come into Manhattan often?" I asked.

"About once a week."

"Where do you live?"

"I have a small room about ten minutes away from here."

I looked at his hands holding the coffee cup. I could imagine them wrapped in a rope halter. I had seen them only an hour before, running up the leg of a horse, searching for a swelling. One of his hands disengaged from the cup. He reached it across the table and placed it down, palm-up. I reached across and placed my hand in his.

I stood just outside my bedroom door watching Charlie Coombs sleep. I had never gone to bed so quickly with a man, no matter how much I had been attracted to him—except for my brief adventure in promiscuity, which really didn't count.

The sex had been very good. We had been very good. Perhaps, I thought, my emerging middle age was going to unflower into a new world of eros. I laughed at my own arrogance.

Two sudden darts of light on the bookcase startled me. Then I smiled. It was Pancho, awake and cruising in his particular fashion. "Go to it," I whispered to him.

I leaned against the wall and closed my eyes. The plaster was cold but I was happy. It had been a long time since I had truly experienced intimacy, that sense that one partner was looking out for the other's pleasure. Charlie was old-fashioned, as he had said. As we made love, he kept telling me how good, how beautiful, how unique I was. It was hokey and charming and ageless and very heady—like a snifter of Napoleon brandy after chocolate cake.

He had, I realized, an ability to give credence to clichés. It was a gift which, oddly enough, I should have had but didn't—because it was what made actresses great, the ability to transcend a silly fiction, a role, and transform it into something that moves an audience to view the world differently.

There was a flash in the darkness. The eyes on the bookcase had vanished. I scanned the pitch-dark bedroom, I heard a furious but nearly silent rustle somewhere.

Then I located Pancho's eyes again . . . and lost them again. Then the eyes seemed to flash off and on like a traffic light that has gone berserk. Finally I realized what was happening. Poor dear crazy Pancho was actually playing with sleeping Charlie Coombs. He was bouncing from one end of the bed to the other

and then to the floor and then to the bookcase, and he was doing it all so swiftly and
quietly and elegantly that the sleeping man
was not disturbed.

It was a good omen. I went back to bed.

The weeks of winter began to grind down. I
landed a small but lucrative part in an avant-
garde German film shot in, of all places, Bay-
onne, New Jersey. My agent started some
"promising" negotiations with "some people" for a possible role as the wife in an Off-
Broadway revival of Pinter's *Homecoming*. I
was asked to teach an acting course at the
Neighborhood Playhouse for their summer
session. And I landed two new cat-sitting as-
signments, one of them an overpaying job
consisting of visiting and feeding a large,
somewhat eccentric Siamese on nine consec-
utive weekends while her owners took a series
of jaunts. Ah, the rich. Anyway, I like German
films, I like Pinter, I like teaching, I love Siamese cats. So things were going quite well.

And Charlie Coombs began to spend at least
two or three nights a week at my apartment.

The magic, as they say, was continuing. It
was odd. We never spoke about what defined
us—the theater or the racetrack. We did speak
passionately and honestly about the stupidest
things: candles, flashlights, cats with tiger
stripes, vegetarian cats, cheeseburgers, boots,
uncles, and the relationship, if any, between
brown eggs and white eggs.

We kept speaking nonsense to each other because we were so enthralled with each other—with the wonder of it all. It was so delicious and crazy that I even enjoyed making coffee for him in the morning.

And so it went. I was finally living the life I should have lived twenty years earlier. I mean, everyone deserves at least one fling at a sublime domestic fantasy.

The bubble, alas, burst on the first Monday in March. It was not Charlie's fault. It was mine. Out of nowhere a face from the past rose up and took me with him.

The bubble burst this way: I was brushing Bushy on the living-room floor. Grooming a Maine coon like Bushy is always a problem, given the thickness of his coat, but the coat itself was a minor chore compared to the cat. Bushy had this peculiar attitude toward being groomed. He acted as if he was about to run away, so one had to hold him firmly. What was worse, he acted as if I was literally torturing him to death.

Once it was finally done and I stared down at my perfectly groomed cat, I had a memory flash so clear and so powerful that I folded my hands like a schoolchild.

I remembered the first time I saw Harry Starobin groom one of his Himalayans.

He had combed the cat out so quickly and so playfully and with such an awesome combination of gentleness, strength, and precision that I had been unable to respond to a question he asked me during the brushing. I had been hypnotized by the perfect harmony of cat and master.

The memory vanished, as they always do, and in its wake came a profound sense of remorse, as if Harry Starobin has risen from the crushed gravel of the Starobin driveway to make a bitter accusation: I, Alice Nestleton, had allowed Harry Starobin to be forgotten.

I could see his craggy, happy, lined face. I could hear him talk. I could see him wearing those green Wellington boots.

The bizarre apparition was so real that I literally started to tell Harry that Jo and I had no choice: we had almost been murdered. But whom was I speaking to? Bushy? Pancho?

The phone started to ring. I ignored it. I went to the bedroom and lay down. When the phone began ringing again, I let it ring. I didn't care at that moment for anyone or anything.

Turning my face into the pillow, I could sense Charlie Coombs's recent presence. He had slept there, we had made love. I turned on my side, feeling bitterly that my life now consisted of making love with Charlie Coombs and cleaning up after Charlie Coombs.

The domestic fantasy was deflating quickly. It dawned on me that a single memory of Harry Starobin had negated what I had considered a profound joy.

As I turned over on the other side, I realized that nothing I had done in my life had provided the intense excitement I had felt during the few days I had spent searching for Ginger Mauch and searching for the source of Harry's secret money. Not making love with Charlie Coombs. Not the theater. Nothing.

I had to do something, I realized. I had to rectify the betrayal. I had to go somewhere.

I sat up. I laughed to myself cynically, remembering the last two lines and the final stage instructions of *Waiting for Godot.*

Vladimir asks: "Well? Shall we go?"

Estragon answers: "Yes, let's go."

The stage direction reads: They do not move.

11

I opened my eyes and found myself staring into Charlie Coombs's eyes. I started to turn away, but his hand reached quickly around my waist and pulled me even closer to him on the bed.

"It's the first time that we've made love and you had other things on your mind," he said.

"Life is harsh," I replied sarcastically, and then added: "What's the matter, Charlie? Didn't you enjoy it?"

He released the pressure of his arm around my waist. I turned away from him.

"Hell, Alice, I train horses for a living, remember? I know when a horse is keeping her mind on her business and when she's not."

I was about to retort angrily that I was not a horse and lovemaking wasn't running—but I said nothing, because he was right. My mind was on other things. I touched him gently on the knee in a kind of apology.

My mind was on Harry Starobin. Maybe I had been wrong about the attempted murder with the pickup truck—maybe the driver had been drunk, as the police speculated.

I looked at Charlie. He still had that hurt expression in his eyes. I moved close to him and tenderly kissed him on the shoulder.

After I had made that gesture, it infuriated me. I edged away from Charlie. What was I doing? It was the same old story again. In all my relationships with men, I had always placated them. I had vowed never to do that again—and there I was, doing it. The moment a little tension had appeared, I had started accommodating his fears.

But I had to defuse the situation—it was too unimportant to keep me engaged with it. I had to defuse it . . . deflect it . . . and to do so, I indulged in a little harmless lunacy. I started to neigh like a horse. Then I asked him if I was now keeping my mind on business like I should. He found that very funny. I found it easy to do. Then we both started acting stupid together, neighing and whinnying like horses. And then we made love again.

We lay there in the dark stillness. Only faint noises from the street could be heard. Even Pancho had ceased his travels. And Bushy was curled up on the far side of Charlie Coombs's pillow.

"Charlie," I said, "I want to ask you a question."

"Ask."

"Suppose I wanted to write a book about that horse you told me about."

"You mean Cup of Tea?"

"Right."

"You didn't even know who he was, Alice."

"Charlie, just imagine I'm writing a book about Cup of Tea. Where do I get information on him—stories, pictures?"

"In both the regular newspapers and the racing press. There have been thousands of stories printed about that horse."

"What is the racing press?"

"I mean papers and magazines that specialize in the racing and breeding of horses."

"Are there many?"

"Sure. There's the *Daily Racing Form, Chronicle of the Horse, Equus, Spur, Thoroughbred Record*—hell, there must be at least fifty."

Bushy, becoming upset because Charlie had raised his voice, contemptuously vacated the pillow and the bed, walking off stiff-legged down the hall toward the sofa in the living room.

"Your cat is telling me something," Charlie said.

"Fool," I said tenderly, and then added, "Go to sleep, Charlie."

I turned away from him and waited to hear the slow, rhythmic breathing which signaled that he had indeed gone to sleep.

For my part, I was filled with anticipatory excitement. I was going to go back in time and find out about that horse called Cup of Tea whose exercise rider had been none other than Ginger Mauch. It was back again to sly Ginger, duplicitous Ginger, dangerous Ginger. Perhaps even dead Ginger. Or perhaps even innocent Ginger—child rider, child lover, fleeing only from a broken heart.

As I lay there in the darkness, I had this tremendous confidence that I had made the right decision. That it was necessary to complete the Harry Starobin file . . . that I had to find Ginger to do that . . . and if I couldn't find her through regular channels, I had to take a different path. Yes—different path—the concept excited me, like it was some kind of Oriental truth or something like that. But it really meant that this time I was starting with a horse—Cup of Tea.

Alice Nestleton was now engaged in writing a book on Cup of Tea. A third career.

It was ludicrous. I stifled a giggle. I was never good at composition, although I had once won a prize in the very early grades for a cat limerick that was so bad it had to win:

> There once was a cat named Lily
> Her face was sweet as Chantilly
>   She milked the cow
>   and herded the sow
> But her kittens were downright silly.

The next morning, Charlie, as always, gave me a long, desperate embrace before he left, as if he would never see me again. I drank my coffee standing at the window. I was happy that Charlie had left early. The whole affair was getting strange. I looked forward to Charlie's visits. I wanted him to sleep over as often as he could. But on the other hand, I had absolutely no desire to share anything with him other than my bed. Perhaps I had been alone too long.

At ten I left the house to begin my new pseudo-career as biographer of a horse called Cup of Tea. I walked uptown toward the Mid-Manhattan Library on Fortieth Street and Fifth Avenue. It was a clear, crisp morning, and I walked easily in a denim dress and wool sweater, my hair loose. Sometimes I slipped into a long-strided gait—what they used to call shit-kicking—the only thing that remained of my childhood on a dairy farm . . . it was the way my grandmother used to walk.

When I reached Thirty-fourth and Fifth I slowed down and began to window-shop. Something was bothering me. My anxiety, though, had nothing to do with where I was going or what I was going to do there. I felt that someone was watching me.

Pausing in front of a store which had an enormous selection of athletic shoes in the window, I turned halfway and saw that I had a clear shot of Fifth Avenue looking downtown.

There were so many people, and none of them were watching me. I must be getting weird, I thought. Even if someone had tried to kill me, I hadn't been looking for Harry's murderer for two months.

Then a flash of color caught my eye: a fishing feather in the rim of a man's hat about two blocks away. He was turning off Fifth as I saw him. Then he and the feather were gone.

Was he the one who had been watching me? How could I be sure? Was it only paranoia induced by the fact that I was once again dealing with the murders of Harry Starobin and Mona Aspen?

I started walking again toward the library. When I reached the entrance I leaned against an outside wall. My hands were sweaty. I didn't feel so good.

I remembered where I had seen a feather like that. At Mona Aspen's place. A hat like that had been worn by her nephew, Nicholas Hill.

I looked downtown quickly. He had not reappeared. Had Nicholas Hill been following me? If so, why? I remembered that when I had spoken to him about Ginger I hadn't liked his attitude or response. He had made me suspicious then.

As I entered the library, though, I had to shake it off. I hadn't been involved in the case for two months. Had he been coming in to New York every day to watch me go to the grocery store? No, it had to be a fluke.

The periodicals librarian, who had never heard of Cup of Tea, told me I should first search the *New York Times Index* before going to the specialty horse magazines.

To my astonishment, I found that there were literally hundreds of references to Cup of Tea. He had obviously been the darling of the *Times*'s sportswriters—an article every three days on average. The horse had even been mentioned prominently in an editorial.

I spent the entire day at the microfilm machine reading articles from the *Times* dealing with the horse's rags-to-riches racing career.

All sorts of innocuous bits of information were scattered throughout the articles: Cup of Tea loved peanut butter spread over a carrot; one of his jockeys was a diabetic; his trainer had been married three times; he won his last three races, before he retired to stud, by a combined total of fifty-one lengths.

I spent two more days on the *Times* and then started on the specialized magazines. I learned much more about Cup of Tea: his stride, his breeding, his training, how he changed leads, how he acted in the barn, what he ate and why.

I really didn't know what I was looking for, but whatever it was, I hadn't found it after six days of intensive research. More important, I had not found a single reference to Ginger Mauch being one of Cup of Tea's exercise riders.

The next week I moved across the street to the main reference library, concentrating on books rather than periodicals. During the years that Cup of Tea had been active as a champion, 1978–1984, dozens of books on horse racing and breeding had been published, and a great many of them at least mentioned him.

My days became very dreary: handing in slips, retrieving books, going through indexes and tables of contents and photo lists and credits. The only reason the stultifying routine was bearable was that I often thought about Harry as I searched the books. Harry would be proud that I had transcended fear and bad faith and returned to the puzzle of his death.

Charlie Coombs, on the contrary, was unhappy. He started complaining about how even on the two nights he slept over, I left him alone with the cats and stayed late at the library. He kept asking me, "Do you really expect me to believe that you're writing a book on Cup of Tea?"

His discomfort started me really thinking about him. I remember one rainy Tuesday when the thought came to me: Where were Charlie Coombs and I going? Did he really love me? Could we live together? I started creating scenarios for both of us, from the ridiculous to the sublime—scenarios of shouting matches and furious lovemaking afterward, of stormy separations and silent reunions.

It was during one of those scenarios that I reached for a book with a beautiful blue cover. The book was titled *Great Thoroughbreds* and was one of those gushy, extravagant items for young girls who become fixated on horses during adolescence. I leafed through the table of contents—a roster of great race-horses: Man of War, Whirlaway, Stymie, Northern Dancer, Secretariat, Ruffian, Forego—it had them all.

Cup of Tea was also there, listed as being on page seventy-eight. I flipped to the page and froze.

In front of me was a picture of Cup of Tea being unsaddled after a workout. A groom was on one side, holding the horse while the trainer did the unsaddling. An exercise rider was crouching next to the horse, fixing something on her boot, helmet in the other hand.

It was Ginger Mauch.

On one side of the horse was a bucket of water, and seated beside the bucket, gazing at Cup of Tea, was a lovely calico cat. The cat had the exact same markings and appearance as the cat I had seen in the photograph Jo and I found in Ginger's abandoned apartment.

Jo Starobin had said that the cat in the photo with Harry was the missing calico barn cat, Veronica.

12

I crept up on the small coffee shop at Thirty-fourth Street just east of Third because I felt in my heart that Jo Starobin wouldn't be there as she had promised. I really don't know why I was doing something so stupid, but all the same, darted a look in the window. I saw her waiting. I felt enormously relieved. When I had called her and told her I wanted to meet her, she had been distinctly unfriendly, talking to me in a polite tone as if we were shopping together in a supermarket. She offhandedly remarked that she had to come into the city to visit the bank vault. Was Thursday okay?

I snuck another look and saw that Jo was bent over, almost as if she was in pain. I kept staring at her through the window, worried now. But when she straightened up, there wasn't really pain on her face—it was despair. It was as if the loss of Harry seemed to crush her from time to time—without warning, without explanation.

I walked inside and slipped into the chair across from her. She had chosen a small table along the wall. She smiled at me—a broad, wonderful smile—and she stretched her hands across the table and I grasped them and we both knew that everything was fine.

When the waitress came over, I ordered an espresso. Jo ordered a cappuccino. We decided to share a piece of deep chocolate cake with cherries.

Jo started to tell me about her train ride into Manhattan, but I broke right into her monologue. I couldn't wait. I pulled out the photograph I had feloniously ripped from the book, and placed it down on the table in front of her. "I've found your barn cat, Jo."

"Veronica? You found Veronica?" Jo asked, astonished, and then leaned over and studied the photograph of Cup of Tea with the exercise rider she recognized as Ginger and the calico cat sitting beside the water bucket.

"Look, Jo," I said, "look at the markings: the exact same as the cat in the photo we saw at Ginger's apartment. You said it was Veronica with Harry."

"Alice, similar markings are very common in calico cats."

"But look at her, Jo," I pleaded.

Jo looked closely, then sat back. "Alice," she said quietly, "this photograph was probably taken around 1981 or 1982."

"So what?"

"Well, Veronica is about three years old now. She was born in 1985. I remember when she was born. It was a small litter."

I had been so excited when I found the picture that I hadn't even considered Veronica's age.

"It could be Veronica's mother," Jo continued, "who was also a calico, if I recall. But how could she have gotten to Maryland? Those cats never left our barn. And Ginger worked in Maryland as an exercise rider before she came to Long Island. No, Alice, it's just another calico cat. And even if it was Veronica's mother—so what?"

I shook my head grimly. I had been so struck by the strange duplication of Ginger and a calico cat that I hadn't considered that someone else would shrug it off. For the past two days I had been adding up facts. Ginger had been an exercise rider for a very famous horse. Subsequently, though, she had become a stable girl on a basically nonworking farm for less than minimum wage. Wasn't that very strange? Now, however, it seemed as though I had gone off half-cocked.

Jo reached across the table, patted me gently on the arm, and said: "It's just a picture of a horse and his mascot, who happens to be a calico cat. All horses have stable companions, Alice. They live with the horses, travel with the horses, play with the horses. Sometimes a horse will go crazy or just lie down and die if its mascot is killed or runs away. Most are dogs or cats, but racehorses have had goats, pigeons, canaries, turtles—and God knows what else—as companions. I once had a carriage horse named Sam who wouldn't step out of his stall unless he was accompanied by a three-legged black cat who lived in the stall with him."

The waitress brought our coffee and placed the piece of chocolate cake equidistant between us with two glistening forks. Jo handed the photograph back to me. I slipped it into my bag.

"It is very good to see you," Jo said.

I smiled and nodded to show her the feeling was reciprocal. Just then I noticed a funny glint in Jo's eye, and I wondered if she knew that Charlie Coombs and I had become lovers. She probably knew, I realized, but was too discreet to say anything unless I brought it up.

"Listen, Alice, can you come out to Long Island tomorrow?"

"Why?"

"There's an auction of Mona Aspen's house furnishings and her paintings and . . . everything. She has a beautiful house."

The change in subject caught me by surprise, and I didn't respond.

"Come out, Alice. You'll love her house. I don't want to go there alone. And besides, Mona would have wanted me to make sure some of her things didn't get into the wrong hands. We can spend some of Harry's money to make sure some of them get a good home. Say you'll come. I'll pick you up at the Hicksville station at the usual time."

"I'll come," I said, caught up by her enthusiasm. I also wanted very much for our friendship to flourish again without the two-hundred dollars a day.

We played with our coffee in silence for a while. Then I asked her, "Have the police found out anything new?"

"Nothing. Whenever I ask them, they say they're still investigating. I ask them what they're investigating. They say they're trying to trace the stolen valuables from a nonexistent inventory list. I don't know who dislikes whom more. But it was my husband who was murdered."

"Have you learned anything new, Jo?"

Jo arched her eyes. "Why would you ask me that, Alice? After all, I took your advice. Remember? You told me I should forget everything and just live."

There was an awkward silence.

"But I couldn't find it," Jo said.

"Find what?" I asked, thoroughly confused.

Jo suddenly began to search frantically under her napkin, under her cup, and then under the table.

"Find what?" I asked again, now concerned about the old woman's bizarre behavior.

Jo relaxed and grinned. "Life, Alice, life. The life you told me to live."

We both laughed so loudly at the joke that the waitress threw us disapproving glances.

*   *   *

Mona Aspen's house was indeed beautiful. Originally an eighteenth-century farmhouse, of which the kitchen, hallway, and dining room were still extant, it had been extended several times, and even its modern wing retained a colonial feel. Jo and I wandered from room to room, staring at the lamps and chairs and rugs, each of which were tagged with the same kind of yellow cardboard on which an auctioneer's code was inscribed. A strange man in a black hat handed each of us a descriptive catalog of the house's contents with prices.

Jo seemed to want to touch everything, to gather everything in, as if she was the sole trusted guardian of her late friend's sensibility. Other people came and went, some greeting Jo, some just walking by with a smile and a nod.

"I'm going to have to sit for a while," Jo said finally spotting an armchair by the fireplace, I guided Jo over to it.

She said, once she was seated, "I keep forgetting that you never were in her house before. You were in the stable area that time. Well, you ought to look at Mona's bedroom. It's really beautiful. And I'll take a nap here."

I hadn't taken three steps away from her when Detective Senay slipped out of an alcove, oddly light-footed for such a large man.

"Well, well, the cat lady," he said. I didn't like the inflection of his voice. And I didn't like the way he had moved right next to me, violating the space that was necessary to maintain a conversation. That, I realized, was one of the reasons I had always disliked him— his willingness to get too close physically. I wondered whether it was a trick of the trade he had learned while interrogating suspects. Did he consider me a suspect?

I smiled and started to move on.

"I made some inquiries about you," he said.

I stopped and turned. "Inquiries?"

"Well," he said, "not really. Let's just say I spoke to some people out in Suffolk County and they said you interfered with a homicide case at Stony Brook."

"No, Detective, you and your friends have it all wrong. I didn't interfere. I just taught them the difference between suicide and homicide. They didn't seem to know the difference."

He didn't like what I said. I don't blame him. But he had started it. "God save us from another dilettante. Tell me, do you have a psychic approach to crime?"

"Right," I said with an equivalent dose of sarcasm. "I solve murders by dissecting birds and reading their innards."

"Birds sound like your speed. Anyway, you may be interested in knowing that two kids in Manhasset tried to sell an eighteenth-century silver tea service that may have come from the Starobin place."

He grinned and started to walk away.

"Wait," I said.

"You want to tell me something?" he asked.

"Yes. I want to tell you that you're crazy if you think Harry Starobin and Mona Aspen were murdered by thieves looking for silverware."

He winked at me as if I was some kind of pathetic eccentric. He strolled off.

It took me a few minutes to compose myself after he walked away, but then I acted on Jo's instructions. I located a long hall which led to a parlor and then to a staircase which, I thought while ascending, had to lead to a dank, dark attic but which instead ended abruptly in an enormous bedroom flooded with light.

It took my breath away. For a moment I longed to be out of the city for good, to live in a room like Mona's. I could envision Bushy and Pancho staring for hours out the room's many windows in feline bliss as the squirrels and the birds danced on the tree limbs before their eyes.

Then I began to inspect the room. The furniture was old and simple and low—oak and cherry wood. The four-poster bed was tiny and fragile, graced by two frayed and no-longer-bright comforters. One of them had a sunflower design.

On the longest wall two oil paintings of horses hung side by side. Between the windows on the shorter walls hung bird prints, mostly waterfowl. One of them was a magnificent print of a loon, done in deep dull purple and black. Like the other rooms in the house, all the items in Mona Aspen's bedroom were also yellow-tagged.

"Pretty, isn't it?"

The voice came from the stairs.

I whirled toward it. Mona's nephew, Nicholas Hill, was standing at the top of the stairs. His sudden appearance frightened me. For a moment I remembered that feathered hat on Fifth Avenue. Or had it been someone else? He wasn't wearing a feathered hat now. He was wearing nothing peculiar except for a very old-fashioned tie with some kind of insignia on it.

I fought back my fear, telling myself it was stupid. Why did I think he would harm me? Did I think he was the one who had driven that pickup truck? Jo had said he was a heavy gambler, but that didn't mean he would murder his aunt. I remembered how grief-stricken he had been after his aunt's death. I remembered how he and Jo had embraced spontaneously over their loss.

He walked into the room toward one of the windows, and his slow, almost lumbering gait kept me on edge. Weren't gamblers supposed to be chipper, nervous little men? For a moment I caught myself measuring his build, wondering if he could hang people on door hooks. But no, that was silly.

If he had been following me that day on Fifth Avenue—if the hat with the feather in it had been his—then maybe he was in the room now to finish something. His hands seemed even more powerful to me than when I had first met him in the barn, cleaning a shovel.

"Do you like those?" he asked pointing at the two horse paintings.

I looked at the paintings again. For the first time I noticed that the space next to one of the paintings was slightly paler. A third painting had obviously hung on the wall there. Had it been sold?

"Yes, I like them, but I doubt if I could afford either one," I replied. "Or those waterfowl prints."

Nicholas nodded and edged closer to the paintings. "My aunt loved these paintings. They were done by Becker. He painted those horses as they were chewing grass in the big field behind the second barn."

"They were your aunt's horses?" I asked.

"Oh, God, no. These are famous racehorses. The first one is Lord Kelvin. The other one is Ask Me No Questions. Both are multiple-stakes winners. Mona just took care of them for a while. One had a bucked shin. The other . . . I forget. Mona nursed them back to health. When they got back to the racetrack, they did nothing but win."

He shoved his hands into his pockets angrily and turned, as if he had committed a felony by reminiscing. "But, as I think I told you before," he continued, "my aunt only liked wounded things. So once they got better, she couldn't care less."

He was very close to me now and I began to

feel apprehensive once again. I heard the sound of footsteps on the stairs. Then the steps reversed themselves and the sounds vanished.

"I have to get back to Jo," I said.

"Then go," he retorted bitterly, as if I was betraying him in some manner. I slipped past him and down the steps.

By the time I finished accompanying Jo throughout the rest of the house, I was totally exhausted. I was sorry I had agreed to come out, even though I knew that Jo had considered it a reinstatement of the friendship. I begged off on Jo's request that I come back to the Starobin house, so she dropped me reluctantly at the Long Island Rail Road station.

As the train left Hicksville station I pulled out a paperback copy of *Romeo and Juliet,* promising myself that I'd use the train ride to give some serious consideration to Carla Fried's offer to play the Nurse. But I got only as far as Act I, Scene ii, before I shut my eyes. I started to doze, then woke, then dozed again.

When the train reached Jamaica, I sat up with a start, looking around desperately. Should I change trains? The conductor assured me it was a through train to Manhattan. I relaxed and realized that while I was dozing I had dreamed about those two horses whose paintings had hung in Mona's bedroom.

What were their names? I reached into my coat pocket and pulled out the auctioneer's list that had been handed to me the moment

I entered the house. I ran down the paintings for sale. There they were, at forty-seven hundred dollars each! *Lord Kelvin* and *Ask Me No Questions.*

What funny names racehorses are given! I was about to crumple and throw the list away when I remembered the empty space on the wall next to the two paintings, where obviously another painting had once hung.

Curious, I looked at the next entry. Superimposed over the name was a rubber-stamped SOLD..

The third painting on the wall was *Cup of Tea.*

13

At noon the next day, Charlie Coombs called. It had been a good week for him. His horses were winning. He wanted to come early and buy me an opulent dinner. I suggested an Indian restaurant in the area. He said that he had never eaten Indian food in his life, but for me he'd do anything.

He came over at four and we sat around and talked to each other, then talked to the cats, then made love, and then went out to eat.

It was one of those small Indian restaurants on Lexington Avenue. The outside was innocuous, but inside was a bizarre profusion of colors: black candles, pink tablecloths, gaily patterned flower plates. Charlie studied the menu carefully, almost compulsively, but he was obviously not really interested in the food.

It was odd. I could understand his relationship to me much better than I could understand my relationship to him. I knew how I impinged on his life. But there it stopped.

Being with me, in any mode, exhilarated him. I turned him into an adolescent.

He wanted to do much more with me than

just make love to me—but he couldn't bring that "more" off. He sensed that I was distant, always distant, and that I would fade away because he was essentially without the substance that bonds permanently. And he needed me forever. I elicited a kind of adolescent inferiority in him, which may or may not have been warranted. I had no idea of his worth even if I could measure such a thing in a man.

He wanted to tell me about his life, his work, his hates . . . but he always pulled back. There was always the thought that I wouldn't truly be interested . . . that I was beyond him . . . thinking other thoughts.

I knew that he loved my body, my face, my long hair, the way I cocked my head before I spoke, the way my face became blank during rapid mood swings which I couldn't control. I knew he wanted to ravage me and protect me at the same time. Poor desperate kindly man. I knew he hallucinated that I was aging with just the right mix of head and heart—like good horses age.

I knew all of that—but I knew little about how his feelings for me impacted on me. And what I did know I could not articulate.

Charlie decided on a dish with lamb and spinach. And a mango drink.

I selected an assortment of breads and small appetizers and avoided a main dish.

It felt good sitting across from him. I appreciated his harmless affectations, one of which was dressing like a hayseed horse trainer—short denim jacket under which were a dress shirt and tie, light-colored flannel pants, and his red sneakers.

"I have some more horse questions for you," I said after we had both ordered and settled in.

"Shoot. That's my business."

"Did you ever hear of a horse called Lord Kelvin?"

"Sure. One of my horses ran against him in Philadelphia Park—the Keystone Stakes, a seven-furlong race. Lord Kelvin won, my horse came in sixth."

"Is there anything peculiar about the horse?"

"Peculiar? What do you mean?"

"I mean like Cup of Tea—a rags-to-riches story."

"That I don't know," Charlie said, adding, "Lord Kelvin was just a good stakes horse, not a 'horse of the year.' I don't even know if he's still racing."

Other couples were beginning to enter the restaurant. A low, gentle buzz surrounded us.

"What about Ask Me No Questions?"

Charlie arched his eyebrows. He was a bit confused by those names coming out of the mouth of a lady who didn't know a thing about the racetrack.

"A pretty horse. A filly, a big gray filly, about sixteen hands high. She used to run in Gulfstream Park, in Florida. A stakes horse, she won a big filly race two years ago when she shipped into Belmont."

"Anything strange about her?"

"Other than her color, nothing at all that I know of. I remember that she didn't do good as a two-year-old; she didn't even break her maiden until she was four years old. But then she turned out real good. Billy Patchen trained her."

I nodded and concentrated for a moment on one of the appetizers which the waiter had just brought. I could sense that my casualness in stopping and starting the questioning was beginning to infuriate Charlie. He always wanted total disclosure. But there was nothing I could do. I was groping for information and I didn't even know what kind of information.

"Should I know more?"

I smiled at him but didn't speak.

"Hell," he said, his irritation rising, "I don't know much. I don't even know where you were all day yesterday. I tried to call you for eight hours straight."

My fork hung in midair. I had never heard him so upset before.

"I guess," he continued sarcastically, "that I'm not supposed to know about the travels of Alice Nestleton. I mean, after all, all we do is sleep together."

I put the fork down and stared at it.

Why had he used the word "travels"?

Had he *known* that I had been out to Long

Island for the auction of Mona Aspen's furnishings?

How could he have known?

Had he really tried to get me for eight hours, or was that just a cover for his knowledge?

What if Charlie Coombs was not who he pretended to be—just my lover? It was odd that he had arrived at the same time—the exact same time—I had begun investigating Harry Starobin's murder. And it was very possible that he had known Ginger Mauch a lot better than he claimed . . . maybe as well as old Harry knew her.

"I'd like you to answer me," Charlie said in a low but threatening voice.

What if the whole affair between Charlie and myself had been orchestrated to keep watch on me?

Or to deflect my interest in the murders?

I could not dispel the growing horror I felt that Charlie Coombs was somehow tied to the whole mess—to the deaths of Harry Starobin and Mona Aspen.

The appetizers lay in a semicircle in front of me. They now looked uniformly loathsome.

"If you don't give me the dignity of a goddamn answer, Alice, I'm walking out of here and you'll never see me again."

I thought: Answer? What was the question?

His voice had started to quake with fury, and perhaps shame.

I couldn't look at him. But I felt him. It was as if he had grown larger and larger; as if he

was hovering over the table—over . . . under
. . . behind. I closed my eyes. Then I could feel
him inside of me . . . in a sexual sense . . . as
if we were making love. I could feel a kind of
synchronicity, like the rhythm of love. For a
moment I hated him more than I had ever
hated anyone in my life. For a moment I loved
him, as if my life hinged on his every move. It
was a crazy few minutes. For the first time
since I had known him, I was reciprocating,
unconsciously, his passion. But it was all
about betrayal.

"Walk," I said, smiling grimly at my fork.
And he did.

14

I stared at the contents of the tall closet in the hallway, the one that contained all my clothes. A depression was coming on, I could feel it—one of those bone-crushing, brain-deadening depressions that turn limbs and will to jelly. I had to get out of the house—to be among people.

Hour after hour I had been analyzing the breakup with Charlie Coombs. But it was too exhausting and too confusing. Of course I knew that I had provoked it by my attitude, and my attitude in turn had originated in my fear and suspicion that he was part of the conspiracy. My attitude alone, however, could not account for gentle, kindly, mature Charlie Coombs's sudden transformation into an abusive, jealous lover.

It was as if someone else had popped out of his body full-blown, like a moth. I didn't want any part of the new Charlie Coombs, on any conditions.

I pulled out of the closet a long white lace Blanche Dubois kind of dress. I pulled from a box on top of the closet a wide-brimmed floppy hat with a black ribbon around the crown. From the bottom of the closet I pulled a pair of red leather shoes.

It was six-thirty in the evening when I stepped out in my antidepression wardrobe, and I had hardly gone a block when the stares of passersby enlightened me to the fact that I was dressed oddly for my age and for the season. It was a young woman's outfit to be worn on a very hot day. The stares didn't deter me. I had a destination, a new restaurant on Twenty-third Street called Brights.

I had never been in there before. I couldn't even conceive of a single reason why I would go in there. But to fight a depression that is about to engulf you, one is forced into very strange alliances.

Brights was done in the latest minimal style; very brightly lit, much space between wood tables. All of it was done in hard-edged style which was designed to do something, but that something was never articulated. And interspersed in all that minimal confusion, like peaches on a desert, were a few garish wall paintings.

When I entered I saw that the end of the bar was crowded with people and the other end was empty. I slipped onto a stool midway between the extremes, removed my hat, and placed it on the stool next to me.

The bartender, a young man with well-coiffed red hair and an open white shirt, placed a napkin in front of me and smiled.

The name of the restaurant was embossed on one corner of the napkin. In fact, everywhere I turned, I saw the name embossed—on the matches, on the stirring sticks, on the clocks.

"A glass of red wine," I said. "Wine keeps ugly depressions an inch away. Brandy is for anxiety, but wine is for depression. It is like a yellow light in the subway.

The wine was served in a glass so huge that a full regular glass of wine would fill only one-third of this jumbo goblet. I sipped it. I listened to the laughter from the crowded end of the bar. I stared out onto the street traffic. I watched the bartender ply his trade.

When I had finished the wine, I began to relax. The danger was receding. As I ordered another glass, I noticed the empty end of the bar was filling up with men and women who obviously were stopping off after work. Who were they? Where did they work? Where did they live? I didn't know. They carried brief cases . . . they carried small posh shopping bags . . . they carried small well-wrapped umbrellas . . . and they carried all kinds of crimes in their hearts. The last notion made me giggle a bit. It was poetic. Crimes in the heart.

Just then two old neighborhood men came in and sat beside me. What were they doing in a posh bar like Brights? Had they lost their way? Did they also need the Brights cure for depression? I removed my hat from the bar stool. One of them gallantly carried the hat to a rack behind the cashier.

I began to concentrate on what to do next. The idea of going back to the libraries with their infernal microfilm machines in order to track down information on Lord Kelvin and Ask Me No Questions as I had done with Cup of Tea made me ill. And besides, Cup of Tea had been a media star. From what Charlie Coombs had told me about the other two horses, that certainly wasn't the case.

I needed someone who knew the racetrack and horses. Charlie Coombs was out of my life now, and besides, he could no longer be trusted. Nor could Nicholas Hill. And Jo, well, I just didn't want the old woman and her new-found money involved anymore.

I stared at the second glass of wine. Was Ginger watching me and laughing at me? I grimaced at the thought.

An argument erupted at one end of the bar, and I heard a woman yell at the man seated beside her. "Don't tell me what he said. I attended the workshop, not you!"

Even as I tried to shut out the quarrel, the word "workshop" stuck in my mind and jangled there. God, it was so nice to hear that word again. How long had it been since I attended a workshop? Then a particular name popped into my head: the Dramatic Workshop. I had studied there under Saul Colin in 1970 or 1971.

Then I remembered Anthony Basillio, their stage designer. He used to bet on horses all the time. I sat back, awed at the strange way things are recalled which seem to have been lost forever. Yes, of course, crazy, wonderful Anthony Basillio would help me. I had met him in a seminar on Brecht at the Dramatic Workshop. The visiting lecturer had been none other than Erwin Piscator, the former director of Brecht's Berliner Ensemble. He was an old, brilliant, difficult man.

Basillio had sat behind me in the seminar. He was tall and skinny, with very bad skin. He was also very funny. Once he brought his cat, Fats, to the seminar in a paper shopping bag, the meanest-looking, most powerfully built alley cat I ever saw. A no-neck, low-slung beastie who was ready to claw. But Anthony told the class not to worry. Fats was really a pussycat. And besides, he was the only cat in Manhattan who could write rock lyrics and pick winners at the racetrack.

I laughed out loud at the memory, then realized the two old men were staring at me. I sipped my wine sheepishly.

The seminars, I remembered, were held at the old Dramatic Workshop studios on Fifty-first Street and Broadway, over the Capitol Theater, and afterward a lot of us used to go to a bar on Eighth Avenue.

It was a time of great ferment in the New York theater world. Radical theater groups of all kinds were rising and falling. The seminar itself had reflected that diversity—academics, Broadway showgirls, directors, stage hands, technicians, famous actors and unknowns, junkies, critics, reviewers. All kinds of people with all kinds of agendas attended. It was that kind of time.

In the bar after the seminar, Anthony used to emote on how he was working on a series of stage designs for *Mother Courage* that would change the way the world perceived Brecht. And sometimes he would have a lot of money on him and buy everyone drinks and cheeseburgers and tell us how he had won the money playing the horses. He used to brag that the only way he could support his theater habit was to make it at the racetrack.

Once he had become very difficult and started a fight, and we were all thrown out of the bar. After the next meeting of the seminar he had apologized and said he often acted stupid because in a past life he had been a racehorse and everyone knew that racehorses were stupid because they got the same food whether they won a race or not.

Basillio would know about Lord Kelvin and Ask Me No Questions.

I paid the bartender and rushed out. A block away I realized I had forgotten my hat. I started to go back, then decided to pick it up another time.

Once in the apartment, I started to pace, trying to remember who had known Anthony Basillio then and who would know where he was now. I grabbed a pad and the telephone book and sat down by the phone.

First, names from the past: actors, actresses, directors, producers, teachers—names I hadn't thought of in years but which now came grudgingly out of the stubby pencil at first, then faster. The names first, then the faces, then the memories.

Ordinarily I would have been too reticent to call these people out of the blue, but now I had no problem at all. Just dial. And dial again. Some were delighted to hear from me. They wanted to make conversation, fill in the years, meet for lunch. Many had unlisted phones and could not be reached. Others gave me numbers of others who might be able to help.

But no one in this widening net of reemerging memories knew what had happened to Anthony Basillio, if, in fact, they had known him at all.

I stared at the clock. I had been on the phone continuously for two hours. My hand was cramped. My throat was hoarse. Each phone call, each opening line, was getting more difficult: "Hello, you may not remember me. My name is Alice Nestleton."

Then the inevitable silence, followed by: "My God— Alice. It has been so long."

At nine-thirty I gave myself six more calls. On the third, I reached Winslow Jarvis, a gay man who had been part of the original Dionysus '69 group on Wooster Street. He said that of course he knew Anthony Basillio, but he hadn't seen him in years. He had heard that Basillio now owned a chain of small Xerox places in the Village and the Lower East Side. He said the stores had a stupid name, something from Brecht.

"Mother Courage?" I asked.

"Right," he said.

I thanked him and hung up. That Anthony Basillio now ran a chain of small copier stores struck me as one of the saddest things I had ever heard in my life.

15

When I was a child, my grandmother had a house cat named Peter who would refuse to eat food off a plate. My grandmother was quite proud of him, saying that because he wouldn't eat off a plate, he could be trusted. It always struck me as odd logic, but that was the kind of feeling I had always had about Anthony Basillio.

Anyway, I started out to find him. The closest branch of the Mother Courage copier chain was on Second Avenue and Third Street. No, the girl behind the counter said, Mr. Basillio's office is in the Sixth Avenue store—at Prince.

I arrived there about eleven-thirty. It was a larger store, and in the rear was a complex of small offices and cubicles. Three or four young men were behind the counter, servicing a continuous flow of customers. The copy machines, all sizes and makes, were humming.

I stood off to one side to distinguish myself from the rest of the customers and finally was approached by one of the clerks, who was wearing an absurd leather apron, as if he were an old-fashioned printer. It was, I recalled, the same kind of apron I had seen Jo wearing on that dismal morning we learned that Mona Aspen had been murdered. But when Jo had worn it I had thought it was a blacksmith's apron.

"Can I help you, miss?"

"I'm looking for Anthony Basillio."

"He's not in."

"Can I wait?"

"To tell you the truth, miss, Mr. Basillio has gone for the day."

"What about tomorrow?" I asked.

"Look, miss, if you really want to see him," the clerk said, exasperated, "you have to get here early. He leaves every day at about eleven for the racetrack, and he doesn't show up again until the next morning."

He paused, smiled at me, and added, "He doesn't have to. He's the boss."

I thanked him and left, promising that I would be back the next morning. He stared at me blankly.

I spent the next twenty-four hours wrapped, metaphorically, in a tourniquet—tense, tight, restricted. I could not proceed without Basillio, and it was necessary to proceed. I went to a movie. I read a few scenes from a Jean Genet play. I groomed Bushy and chased Pancho. I thought of Charlie Coombs with regret and then anger; of Harry Starobin with a kind of bitter adolescent longing; and of Jo Starobin with warmth. It was an exhausting, nerve-racking day that vanished very slowly.

At eight-forty-five the next morning, I stood once again in front of the counter of the flagship Mother Courage copier shop. The clerk with the leather apron remembered me, raised one section of the counter, and waved me through—pointing to a specific office in the back. The door was open. A man sat at a desk, his chair turned to the window. Hearing my footsteps, he wheeled around.

"My God, the Swede!" He jumped out of his chair.

I smiled and held out my hand. He had always called me Swede after he found out I was from Minnesota, even though I had told him a hundred times that I wasn't of Swedish descent. It was just one of his stereotypical Hollywood affectations.

Basillio really hadn't changed at all, except for his graying hair and worse posture. He was still thin. His skin was still bad. His smile was still wicked, as if he was perpetually contemplating some kind of mayhem.

"Look, Alice," he said in a mock-serious tone, putting his arm around me and guiding me to a chair, "I refused to sleep with you then and I refuse to sleep with you now. So, do you still want to visit, or are you too broken-hearted?"

I laughed until the tears welled up in my eyes. He represented an old and treasured time for me—when the theater had been much more than just a precarious profession, when it had still been a kind of religious vocation.

"I see your name around, Swede, but not all that much."

"No, not all that much," I agreed.

"But at least you're still in it . . . and you never went show biz," he noted with an appreciative smirk.

"I tried," I replied. And we both laughed hugely at this most hoary of all acting-class insults. We felt an enormous kindness toward each other.

"Remember what the master said," Anthony cautioned.

"Which master?"

"Which master? There's only one, Swede. Bert Brecht. He said, 'Don't let them lure you into exhaustion and despair.' "

"I see they haven't."

"Nor will they," he affirmed.

"Tony, I didn't come here to talk to you about Brecht or the theater. It took me a hundred calls to find you. I need help."

Basillio's eyes narrowed at the word "help."

"I need information on horses."

"Horses?" he asked, astonished.

"Racehorses."

"You mean you want me to give you tips?"

"No. Information on their personal lives."

"Whose personal lives?"

"The horses'."

"Racehorses don't have personal lives. They run and they die."

"Cup of Tea did."

"Cup of Tea was special."

"I'm writing a book on Cup of Tea," I said, using that convenient fabrication, "and I need information on his contemporaries. Not betting information—other kinds. I just broke up with a trainer named Charlie Coombs."

"I know of him," Basillio said, interrupting.

I continued, "So now that Charlie is gone from my life, I need someone who can talk horse talk."

"Maybe, Swede, you'll just have to hop into bed with another trainer. I mean, they're the only ones who really know horses' breeding and conformation and potential. All I know is what I pick up from other gamblers—crazy stuff that may or may not be true. Like how the horse can't run if the temperature gets over eighty degrees or if he likes beer in his feed or that the horse is really crazy unless a lady jock climbs on his back. That kind of stuff."

"That's what I want, Tony," I said, realizing that my lies were now spiraling. Charlie and I had never talked about horses—except for the first and last times we were together.

He whirled around on his chair. "Swede, if there was one woman on earth on whom I would have happily bet my wife, my kiddies, and all my copying stores that she would have never gotten involved with the racetrack, it was you. You were always too elegant, too goddamn classy. Or maybe, at most, a three-day trip to Saratoga in August with a rich lover to watch the horses run in between ballets."

He was starting to sound like my ex-husband.

"Believe me, Tony," I said, "it's not a willing involvement. This book I'm writing is a debt."

"Bookmakers?"

"No, the dead."

"The dead?" he repeated softly.

"I want to find out all the information I can about Lord Kelvin and Ask Me No Questions."

"Forget the first horse."

"Lord Kelvin? Why?"

"He's dead. Lord Kelvin was killed in a freak vanning accident in Pennsylvania about a year ago. I know because I met this guy at the track who told me he saw a small notice about it in a Philadelphia paper. He mentioned it to me because we both had made some money on that horse."

I wondered why Charlie had never told me that when I asked him about Lord Kelvin. Was it possible he didn't know?

"That leaves Ask Me No Questions," I noted.

"I've seen her run," Anthony replied. "Look, just give me a few days."

I wrote my number on his desk pad. I remembered, as I was writing, that I had done the exact same thing at the racetrack when I first met Charlie. "Thanks," I said, standing up.

"Wait, Swede," he called out with a touch of panic in his voice.

I turned back to him.

"Aren't you going to tell me how sad this all is, Swede? The Mother Courage copier shops instead of the Mother Courage stage sets? Aren't you going to say how goddamn pathetic it all turned out?"

"No," I replied. There was silence. "You told me once in a bar, after a seminar," I reminded him, "that when all was said and done, gambling was your only passion."

"I lied," he said.

I wanted to leave. I didn't know what to say. Basillio picked up on my discomfort and said, "Remember when I brought my cat, Fats, to the seminar in a shopping bag?" We both laughed so loud the customers in the front of the store were startled and peered past the counter toward us.

I went home and waited for Basillio to call. That he would call, that he would give me information I required, was never in doubt. He was a blast from the past, and the past is always good.

Sure enough, he called me two days later. He said he was going to the racetrack, but he would meet me in front of the Plaza Hotel at eight that evening and buy me seven dozen littleneck clams, three dozen cherrystones, nine brandies, and a piece of cheesecake in his favorite place—the Oyster Bar.

"Can't we meet in a coffee shop some-where?" I asked.

His voice was happy, playful, manic: "Don't provoke me, Swede. It's the Plaza or nothing."

At seven-forty-five I was standing in front of the Plaza Hotel. I felt stupid and ill-at-ease; I had provoked another male into adolescent gestures. I was wearing jeans and a sweater, just to be perverse, I imagine.

He arrived a half-hour late, flushed, excited. Grabbing my arm in a tight grip, he led me up the steps of the hotel, across the lobby, and then into the Oyster Bar by the back entrance, where we were seated by a man who looked like he had survived prewar Vienna only by the skin of his domed head.

"Look at the bar, Swede. Don't you love it? It's square. I mean, did you ever see another bar with corners?"

Once we were sitting across from each other, I could tell that he had been drinking before he met me.

"How did you do at the racetrack?"

"I lost heavy."

"Easy come, easy go," I said by way of a gentle criticism.

He smiled at me. He ordered clams and brandy and ale. "So," he said after it was all settled, "what I found out, you probably already know."

"Try me," I said.

"Right. Ask Me No Questions was a big,

hard-running gray filly. Not much breeding, but she ended up a multiple-stakes winner."

"Like Cup of Tea," I said, remembering that Charlie had told me there was absolutely no similarity.

"Sort of, but not really," Anthony hedged, staring at the two plates of beautiful little-necks and one plate of cherrystones. He began to prepare them carefully—lemon, horseradish, a tiny dollop of hot sauce.

He explained, "No one ever went from no-where as far and as fast as Cup of Tea. He went from a dirt track to become the world's champion grass horse and sire. Ask Me No Questions never started that low or went so high. She won grade-two stakes at best, not the Arlington Million like Cup of Tea."

"But something did happen. I mean, there *was* a transformation, wasn't there?"

"Right. Something sure as hell happened. She lost her first twelve races. They sent her back to the farm. She came back as a four-year-old, lost six more races; then went back to the farm with another injury. The next time she raced, four months later, she won an allowance race by ten lengths at odds of sixty-five to one. And she kept on winning."

I sat back, exhausted suddenly by the realization that I had at least put one firm piece into the puzzle. "Thank you," I said.

He grinned at me wickedly and pushed the clams across the table. The one I ate was cold, tart, delicious.

"Do you want to see her?" he asked.

"Of course! Can I see her?" It had never dawned on me that I would have access to Ask Me No Questions.

Triumphantly he pulled a small piece of paper out of his shirt pocket, unfolded it, and slid it across the table to me the same way he had slid the clams. It read: "James Norris Stables, Far Hills, New Jersey."

"They retired Ask Me No Questions to become a brood mare. But there was something wrong with her. She couldn't conceive, and when she finally did, she couldn't deliver a live foal. So they sold her to that stable in Far Hills. They're going to make a Grand Prix show jumper out of her—you know, going over seven-foot fences for ten thousand dollars first-prize money contributed by Volvo or BMW. For all I know, she's a jumper by now."

"You told me what I need to know," I said thankfully.

"I wish you'd stop thanking me, Swede. After all, I'm not a happily married man and you're going to damage what remains of my libido. Besides, you don't think for a minute that I believe all that nonsense about you writing a book on Cup of Tea."

I was barely listening to him now. An absurd little ditty was bouncing around my head:

> Three little racehorses
> Hanging on a wall

Two hung straight
But the third took a fall

I wasn't finished with Anthony yet. "Did anyone mention to you an exercise rider named Ginger Mauch?"

"You mean someone who used to ride Ask Me No Questions?"

"Yes."

"Never heard the name. But, then again, exercise riders are anonymous unless they're name jockeys and doing a favor for the trainer. Is this Ginger a jockey?"

"No," I answered, trying a cherrystone this time, remembering that Dr. Johnson used to feed oysters to his cat. I started wondering if Bushy and Pancho would like clams, speculating how best to remove them in their half-shells from the Plaza.

Basillio started a monologue about how the racetrack was the closest thing around to Brecht's conception of theater. The brandy was obviously getting to him.

"How do I get out to Far Hills?" I asked him.

"By car. Take the George Washington Bridge. Then some kind of highway you pick up there—84 or 80 or 287—I forget which."

I began to look around for the first time since I had sat down. There were only out-of-town faces, like mine had been so many years ago.

"Do you know what, Swede?" Basillio

asked, now desperately trying to get a waiter's attention for coffee.

"What?"

"I think you're going to ask me to do you another favor. So, before you ask, I'm going to offer it. Not because I'm a good guy or anything like that, but because it was so damn wonderful to see you again and I don't want it to be another seventeen years before we see each other again. So, I'll take you to Jersey. No big deal. I live in New Jersey—Fort Lee. I'll take you to see Ask Me No Questions."

"You going to interview the horse with a tape recorder?" Basillio asked, chuckling.

I nodded absentmindedly, staring out the window of the late-model Pontiac. Actually, I didn't know why I was driving out to see the horse. But I was going. For that was the way the thing was developing. One tiny, stupid step at a time. Ask Me No Questions was a real live thing that I could see and touch, not a painting on a wall or a photograph in a book. I was going to see a horse.

Basillio started asking me theater questions—about old friends and colleagues: Where was L? What about R?

I answered the best I could. The traffic was thinning. The motion of the car soothed me. Basillio was a good driver, fast and safe. Snatches of a poem I had studied in school came to me: "That's my Last Duchess painted on the wall." Was it Browning?

A little more than an hour after we crossed the George Washington Bridge, we pulled up to the Norris stables. The place was a large complex with indoor and outdoor rings and dozens of young girls standing around with riding helmets and whips. There were jump courses on which classes were being held, and a steady stream of lathered horses being led from ring to stable.

"Well, it isn't Belmont Park," Basillio said.

We parked the car and entered the main office.

A tall, elderly man wearing a sheepskin vest greeted us. I proceeded with my fiction, slanting it a bit: I was writing a book on lady racehorses who had beaten the boys. I wanted to take a look at Ask Me No Questions, who had done just that many times.

The man smiled and said, "She's going to beat the boys in the jumping ring also."

Basillio whispered in my ear, "You keep changing your story about what kind of book you're writing. Why don't you stick to one story?"

I ignored his comment. The elderly man leafed through some index cards and then said, "She's being schooled now on course number three. Why don't you take a walk over?"

He led us to a window and pointed out the path to the course.

As we headed that way, I began to search

the faces that passed us. Would Ginger be here? Was that why I had come?

When we reached the course, a large gray horse was being led over very small jumps at a very slow pace. Most she took easily, hesitating just a bit when she was forced to jump after coming out of a tight turn. The girl on her back encouraged her, crooned to her, patted her neck constantly. Then the rider pulled up, slid off, and started to lead Ask Me No Questions out of the ring.

"What a beautiful lady," Basillio whispered in awe.

I could not respond. I, too, was mesmerized by the rippling, delicate, gathered beauty of the mare. But I felt something else: I was finally about to make contact in some way with the ashes of Harry Starobin.

My hands were trembling as I told my story to the rider, a chunky girl of about twenty, who then invited us both back to the barn, a bit proud that someone was going to put Ask Me No Questions in a book.

As we all walked back together, Ask Me No Questions playfully swung her head and hit Basillio on the chest.

"She's paying me back for the time I bet against her," he said.

As we reached the entrance of the large barn where she was stabled, As Me No Questions suddenly stopped, planted her feet, and would go no farther. The girl smacked her on the rear end. But Ask Me No Questions would not budge.

"Hell," said the girl, "I forgot that she won't go in until Marjorie comes out."

"Who is Marjorie?" Basillio asked.

The girl laughed. "You'll see. Oh, here she comes."

As we waited there, sweat started beading on my face. It will be Ginger, I thought, here she comes!

"There's Marjorie," the girl said happily, and the horse moved forward.

Lumbering out in front of the barn, yawning, was a large, beautiful calico cat.

16

I showed the wine bottle to Bushy, as if I was a waiter and the cat was a patron. Bushy ignored it. I opened it quickly and poured myself a glass of good Bordeaux—a St. Emilion.

The wine was for my confusion. I sat down on the sofa, my legs drawn tightly together. The search had ended in a calico cat named Marjorie strolling out of the barn. Ginger had not been there. Of course she hadn't. Why had I ever thought she would? Only a calico cat. And a different calico cat from the one in the Cup of Tea photo, which in turn had been a different calico cat from Veronica the barn cat, according to Jo. Just a calico cat. A horse's mascot.

I went into the kitchen, opened the refrigerator, took out some St. André cheese, and spread it on a rice cake. Pancho was high on a cabinet, staring down at me. He loved cheese.

I walked back to the living room and ate the snack, staring out the window onto the street.

"Poor Ginger," I muttered. I put the wineglass down on the sill, stiffening a bit. Why had that popped out? Lately I had found myself muttering out loud from time to time. But usually it was "poor Harry" or "poor Jo." Why in God's name would I suddenly be feeling sympathy for Ginger Mauch. Ginger was the enemy. Wasn't she?

It was suddenly apparent to me that Ginger was probably just a frightened girl. She had been running from the murderers before they caught up with her.

The next morning, as I made coffee, I conjured up an image of a short, chunky red-haired young woman, physically strong, with a nervous way of speaking, dressed in work clothes. Where would Ginger run to?

Not to the racetrack. It was too well-regulated. Everyone knew everyone. People walked around with identification badges.

Not on Long Island. Too many people knew her.

She might be a thousand miles away, in some Midwest or Southern hamlet, but in that case I'd never find her. I had to proceed on the assumption that she had melted into the one place where her face was one of millions—the perfect camouflage. She was right here in Manhattan. In New York City she would be just another young woman seeking a job.

And where would an exercise rider with a lifelong passion for horses get work?

My hand holding the coffee cup began to shake ever so slightly. I knew where Ginger would be working. Of course. At the last remaining riding stable in Manhattan—at Claremont on West Eighty-ninth Street.

I had been there many times when I first came to New York. I used to take long walks on the bridle path in Central Park and follow the horses and riders home to the stable, marveling at how the experienced horses could pick their way gingerly through the traffic-choked, double-parked streets once they left the park.

I dressed quickly, without thinking, and only after I was fully dressed did I realize that I was wearing the clothes I usually wore only to acting classes—jeans and an old sweatshirt on which was printed PROPERTY OF ATHLETIC DEPARTMENT/UNIVERSITY OF VIRGINIA. I never knew where or how I had obtained that sweater—it had just appeared.

My instinctive clothes selection was a good omen, I thought. One always attempted to diminish one's natural beauty in acting classes, since it was looked upon as fakery. The ability to go deep inside a character was what was treasured. And wasn't I doing that? Wasn't I going inside of Ginger's head?

I was catching a character, a role—I was intuiting another's movement. I was a bloodhound . . . a choreographer . . . a nonsensical forty-one-year old actress on the move. Chuckle. You know what they say: Bedouins sharpen their vision by painting the whites of their eyes blue.

I folded the only photograph of Ginger I had—the one with Cup of Tea and an unidentified calico cat—and placed it carefully in my bag. Then I left the apartment, cautioning the cats against any bizarre behavior, took the Third Avenue bus to Seventy-ninth Street, and walked west through the park.

The riding stable had not changed. On either side were the same crumbling brownstones. There was the same small, low-ceilinged ring with posts scattered throughout. The same treacherous ramp led from the ring to the stall area on the second floor. The office area was still as crowded as a subway car, even though it was late-morning on a weekday, with children, parents, instructors.

I finally cornered a man who seemed to have managerial responsibilities and gave him the current fiction: I was writing a book about the great racehorse Cup of Tea, and I had learned that one of his exercise riders was now working in his stable.

The man, who wore a whistle around his neck and riding boots in which white carpenter jeans were stuffed, folded his arms impatiently, as if I was a saleswoman about to launch into a long pitch. "That's news to me," he said in a heavy foreign accent which I could not identify.

"Her name is Ginger Mauch."

"No Ginger Mauch works here."

"Well, maybe she's a groom."

"No groom named Ginger Mauch works here. No instructor either."

I pulled the picture out and shoved it under his face, signifying but not saying that she might be working under a different name. It was too gloomy in the ring to see the photo clearly. Angrily he took the photo and strode to the stable entrance, flooded by the morning sun. I followed.

He stared at the picture, then handed it back. "No," he said, "I've never seen that woman here, and I've worked here for the last nine years."

I walked out of the riding stable so bitterly disappointed that my lower lip started to quiver like a child's. It never had really occurred to me that Ginger wouldn't be there. I knew she would be there. The doors of perception had shut on my arrogance like a steel trap.

I walked to Broadway, found a coffee shop, and collapsed in a booth. I ordered a cup of tea and a piece of coconut custard pie.

Everything connected with the murder of Harry Starobin seemed to recede . . . to have taken place fifty years ago. I wanted to push it even further back . . . to get away . . . to go to the shore . . . to the mountains . . . anywhere. I wanted out of those tiny compulsions

which were leading me from one cipher to another.

"Poor Alice," I mocked myself, "too old to
really enter a part."

I ate the pie slowly and doggedly, deter-
mined to get some energy. I sipped the tea.
When the coffee shop began to fill up with a
lunchtime crowd, I left, contemplating for a
moment a cab . . . then deciding it would be
best to walk.

I went back into Central Park and walked
downtown. It was a glorious spring day. Everyone was out walking, jogging, bicycling.
Even the homeless derelicts, huddled among
the trees, seemed less desperate, less aggressive than usual.

When I reached the Tavern on the Green, I
stopped and stared, discomfited, tense. Years
ago I had eaten brunch there with my husband on a Sunday morning. The marriage was
already in the last stages of dissolution and
the brunch had become ugly. The dialogue
between us was late-Gothic-bitter—and cen-
tered around that most absurd of things,
cream for the coffee:

He: I want half-and-half for my coffee. They
gave us plain milk.

Me: Ask the waiter.

He: You ask the waiter. He keeps smiling at
you.

Me: Are you jealous?

He: He can have you. All I want is the half-
and-half.

I wondered why I had always remembered that stupid exchange—word for word, nuance by nuance.

I exited Central Park at Columbus Circle and turned east onto Central Park South. There were the carriage horses lined up in their accustomed spot, waiting for tourists. Their drivers, bizarrely outfitted, sat high up on their boxes, calling out to people passing.

I kept well clear of them; I was sick of horses.

The Plaza came into view. It was where I had had the clams with Anthony Basillio. He had been a good friend.

Suddenly there was violent barking. A woman held a dalmatian on a leash and the dog was pulling at it violently and barking at a big white carriage horse parked by the curb, whose nose was hidden in a feed bag.

The woman holding the dog was yelling apologies to the driver. The driver just smiled and nodded her head. The horse seemed totally unconcerned.

I started to cross Central Park South to continue in a downtown direction. The light was with me.

I stopped suddenly and let the light change.

My heart was beginning to jump, to beat with a funny little flutter—quickly, lightly, but pronounced.

My hand grasped my shoulder bag tightly and then released it.

The city became silent. I was frozen in time and space.

The carriage driver behind the big white horse was Ginger Mauch.

17

The watch on the waiter's thin wrist read two-twenty. It seemed to be a very old watch. Maybe it had been his grandfather's. Maybe he was an out-of-work actor and he had come to New York from Minnesota, from a dairy farm, and the watch was the only rural memento he had left. How could a watch be a rural memento? Stupid thoughts.

I had been sitting in the outdoor café on the corner of Sixth Avenue and Central Park South for more than an hour. I had kept my eyes glued on the carriage with the big white horse.

The carriage was moving slowly but inexorably westward, toward me. Each time a carriage was hired, the others moved up—like a taxi line in front of a hotel.

An untouched Bloody Mary was in front of me. The waiter was bothersome, continually asking me if I wanted anything else. Business was slow. It was just a bit too early in the spring for café sitting.

There could be no doubt that the carriage driver was Ginger Mauch. Her hair was short

now and dyed brown. But it was her. I had
seen her in the flesh three times before this:
once when I arrived by taxi at the Starobins'
place on that terrible day; once when we were
being questioned by the police; and once that
same night, when I had stumbled on Ginger
weeping behind the cottage.

No, this was not a mistake. This was real.
This was Ginger.

In retrospect it was all so logical. Ginger had
taken care of the old Starobin carriage horses.
Of course she would seek work in Manhattan
with carriage horses.

The longer I sat there, the more frightened
I became. It wasn't physical fear of Ginger; it
was something else. Something to do with the
fear that even finding Ginger would yield only
another dead end . . . a wall . . . a blinking image of a calico cat.

Ginger's carriage moved another space. I realized I would have to make my move soon. I
placed a ten-dollar bill on the table in a manner which mutely showed that the waiter
could keep the change from the drink—a very
substantial gratuity. The sight of the ten-
dollar bill calmed the waiter; he stopped
hovering about me.

What happens if I wait too long and someone else hires the carriage? The thought pan-
icked me.

I left the café swiftly, walked to the corner,
and waited for the light to change.

Then I crossed the street to the carriage side

and waited, turned away from the line of view. It suddenly occurred to me that since I was wearing my acting-class garb, Ginger would never even recognize me.

It was only by chance, instinctively, that I had selected that particular garb. In fact, everything had ended up without reason. I had found Ginger by chance, and only by chance. My reasoning, my "getting into the part," had gotten me nowhere. It was a chance walk at a chance time in a chance place—and a dalmatian dog barking for no bloody reason.

The absurdity of it all gave me strength.

I whirled around, walked ten steps, and was about to climb up into the carriage.

I froze before the carriage steps. Ginger's head was in repose.

I turned and walked quickly away, five steps, ten steps, then stopped. Not the carriage. Not the carriage now. It was wrong. It was childish. What was I going to do in the carriage? What was I going to say? Where were we going to ride?

It wasn't a confrontation that was needed. It was information. Where was she living? Whom was she talking to?

I took ten more steps away from her. What if Ginger wasn't a victim? What if she wasn't running but was pursuing?

I walked toward the low wall that separated the sidewalk from the park. I turned. A couple had climbed into Ginger's cab. They were pulling away. Fine. Ginger would be back to deposit her fares after the ride was over.

I leaned against the wall and waited. From where I stood I could dimly see the waiter in the street café I had vacated.

Ten minutes. Twenty minutes. She and her carriage would be back. Thirty minutes. Sixty minutes. The big white horse poked his nose out of the park, moving leisurely toward the line again. Ginger pulled the carriage up about ten yards from me and helped her fare down graciously.

Then she climbed up again and started to move. But this time she didn't rejoin the line. She pulled out into the street and headed west on Central Park South.

She was going back to the stable. She was through for the day. I started to walk, easily keeping her in view, staying as far away from the curb as I could. Her pace was painfully slow, as if she was allowing the horse a leisurely stroll.

The horse and carriage turned south on Broadway and then west again on Fifty-fifth Street, then south on Eleventh, and then stopped in front of a long, low, decrepit stable in front of which were dozens of broken-down horseless carriages. Ginger climbed down and led the horse and carriage inside. I could see her disengaging the horse from the carriage and leading him into a stall. I moved away from the stable and waited near the corner, in front of a busy taxi garage.

She was in there forty minutes. When she came out she walked briskly to a white stone house on Forty-ninth Street and Ninth Avenue.

I climbed the stairs into a cramped, filthy lobby. There were sixteen plastic buttons and under each one a nameplate. There was no Ginger Mauch. What name was she using? I didn't know, but it had to be one of the newer plates. There were three of them: L & H Martinez; Jon Swan; M. Lukas. It had to be Lukas. Ginger Mauch was now M. Lukas. I walked out of the lobby and down the steps. Right next to the building was a small bodega. I walked inside, ordered a container of black coffee, and sipped it dourly, standing inside the store, by the front window.

What was I waiting for? I had postponed the confrontation in the carriage. And now I was doing the same thing: waiting . . . making excuses. Now was the time to confront her. Now was the time to ask her all those questions I had stored up in my head: about Harry; about those damn calico cats; about Veronica the barn cat; about Cup of Tea and Ask Me No Questions; about her life on the racetrack and her life with the Starobins; about whom she was running from or running to.

Why was I equivocating? What was I afraid of? Why couldn't I confront her? What was the point of the whole investigation . . . what was the point of tracking her if I couldn't finish it up?

The coffee was horrible—bitter, with a funny taste, as if someone had poured some kind of syrup into it. I dumped the container into a carton of trash. But I stayed where I was and stared out onto the street. Children in parochial-school outfits were talking in front of the bodega. I could hear them dimly, but their words made no sense. Then I realized they were speaking in Spanish. I started to laugh at myself. I walked out of the bodega, up the steps of the house, into the small lobby, and pressed my finger hard against the M. Lukas bell. There was no answer. Maybe the bells didn't work. The landlord had obviously long since given up on the building. Realizing this, I pushed at the lobby door. It opened easily. The lock was still in the door but was totally corroded. I cursed myself for not trying the door the first time.

M. Lukas lived on the third floor. Up I went, slowly, trying to think of opening lines that would get me inside that apartment.

A burly man walking down the stairs greeted me warmly. A woman passed me and didn't say a word. The ceilings above the stairs were filthy. Chips and pieces of paint seem to flutter down in a steady stream, jarred loose by footsteps on the stairs.

The first door I saw when I reached the third floor was 3E. Was this M. Lukas? The door was ajar. At the top of the landing I stared at the open door and felt an incredible sense of déjà vu. When Jo and I had traced Ginger to her apartment in Oyster Bay Village, we had found the same thing. The door ajar. Ginger gone. Was there a back door to the building? I wondered, cursing myself.

I stopped at the doorway. "Ginger, Ginger Mauch?" I called into the opening. The sound of my voice was strange to me, as if someone else was calling.

There was no answer.

I pushed the door open and stepped inside. "Ginger," I called agai , more softly.

The apartment was a studio. And it had been ripped apart. Clothes and books and papers were flung all around. Things had been shattered. A tiny kitchen had been totally ransacked. The apartment stank of something I couldn't identify.

Then I noticed that the bathroom door was closed.

I walked to it swiftly, my feet crunching objects on the floor. I pushed the door open with my foot.

And then I sank to my knees. Ginger Mauch was sitting in the rusted bathtub. The red roots in her brown-dyed hair were visible. Torrents of blood had flowed and dried on her naked body. The cut across her throat was a jagged white road.

I remained kneeling on the floor, half in and half out of the bathroom. I knew what I had to do. Stand up. Go to the phone. Call the police. But I was paralyzed.

I started to cry for Ginger. Not because she

was dead, for death seemed to be irrelevant in that room. Because she had suffered. Because she had felt pain. Because some animal had slit her throat. I could see her as I had seen her that first time, in the cold gleaming morning, from a distance, brushing the aged horse on the Starobin farm.

I stopped sobbing. I crawled out of the bathroom and found myself surrounded by her trashed belongings. What had they been looking for?

A heap of books had been pulled off the bookcase and lay in a crazy pyramid. One of them caught my eye. I knew it. I was staring at a copy of the book I had found in the library, the one containing a photo of Ginger and Cup of Tea. The thought chilled me. My eyes swept in fear around the room. Not for her killer, but for the calico cat. There was none. Poor Ginger. The book was probably a precious memento.

I reached out and pulled it to me. As I did, a piece of old thick cardboard slid out. It was taped around the edges to thicken it, like boys used to tape their baseball tickets.

I found myself reading some kind of list or inventory on each side. The letters and numbers were indecipherable, written in red and black crayons and smudged.

But I knew one thing. I was staring at something written by Harry Starobin. His scrawl had been indelibly imprinted on my brain, after sorting through hundreds of his papers at Jo's request.

Harry Starobin and Ginger Mauch had been part of some kind of conspiracy, and I had found the code book.

I was awakened by strange sounds. I stared at the clock in my bedroom. It was one in the morning. I had slept almost seven hours. The police, I knew, would have responded to my call in minutes and Ginger was by now a statistic, her apartment contents cataloged, her walls and furniture swept for prints.

Those strange sounds that woke me were the cats. They wanted to be fed. I climbed slowly off the bed, the back of my neck and shoulders stiff.

After I fed them, I made myself a cup of coffee and then went into the living room, where the strange piece of taped cardboard lay on the long table.

I sat down and stared at it.

The front was a fourteen-line list:

78/TTQQCC
79/TTQCCC
80/TQQQCC
81/TQCCC
82/TC
82/QQCC
83/TTTQCC
83/TQQC
84/TQQCC

85/TQC
85/TTQC
86/QCCC
87/QCCC
88/TTTTTCC

It was obvious that the numbers were years: 1978–1988. There was only one line for each year except for the years 1982, 1983, and 1985—where there were two entries each.

But what were those funny capital letters after each year—T or Q or C?

They must mean something. They must be important. Ginger had carried them with her during her travels.

Bushy sauntered into the living room and hopped up on the sofa, quite content with his meal.

Pancho flew by once, paused, stared at me, and continued his journeys.

I was chilly. I wrapped a blanket around my shoulders.

I stared at the markings on the cardboard again. It was obvious that Harry was tallying something that happened in each year. It was an inventory . . . a count . . . like someone saying an apple tree produced eighty barrels of apples in 1986. Or a farm produced thirty barrels of peaches, twenty of plums, ten of pears, in a given year.

But what had he been counting?

I leaned back and closed my eyes, thinking

of Harry. What had defined him? Humor. Kindness. Boots. Animals. Cats. Horses.

But he didn't grow any of those things. He didn't produce.

Harry wasn't a breeder of anything. His farm was totally nonfunctional.

Except . . . except . . . except for the Himalayans. No, he hadn't bred them.

Except for the barn cats. Jo had said there were always litters of barn cats. Veronica had vanished with her litter.

I stared at the letters.

Why would Harry list in coded form litters of barn cats over the years? And what did the letters mean?

Of course! I flung my hand up to accentuate my own stupidity. T stood for tom—a male cat. Q stood for queen—a female cat. Old names that people didn't use anymore.

My fingers were trembling ever so slightly.

According to my analysis, in 1978, the first year of the inventory, the barn-cat litter consisted of two male kittens, two female, and two Cs.

But what was C?

Calico. A delicious chill went right through me. I had broken the stupid code.

Then I pulled back my enthusiasm. If my analysis was correct, there were calico cats in each litter, in most years more than one, and in some years more than half the litter.

That was impossible. I had read a lot about calico cats over the years.

There are only three multicolored cats, found only in females—blue cream, tortoiseshell, and calico. Calico is the most difficult to reproduce.

To obtain a calico, one breeds a male with a dominant white color to a tortoiseshell female. The white male is crucial because calico is really only tortoiseshell plus the color white. White, in fact, is the dominant color of the calico cat.

If the mating is successful, a calico female may appear in the litter—possibly even two.

But over the long run, calico is very hard to produce. The accepted probabilities are one calico female out of every seventeen kittens.

I stared down at the list again. How could Harry have bred so many calico cats in each litter of barn cats?

Was Harry a magician? Had he somehow done what cat breeders considered impossible?

I turned the cardboard over. This side contained dozens of entries, many of them faded.

Among the ones I could make out were:

RS/87C
NA/83C
LBD/86C
COT/78C
LK/81C
ANQ/82C

FG/84C
GB/84C
R/79C
BB/79C

The second part of each entry I now understood. C meant calico; 84 meant the 1984 litter; 84C meant a calico cat from the litter in
1984.

But what did it refer to? What referred to it?
What did FG/84C mean?

It was the LK/81C entry I focused on most.
For some reason it infatuated me. The letters
LK meant something to me, or reminded me
of something.

I began to make up possibilities. Ladybird.
LK. Ladybird in Kansas. LK. Larry Koenig.
Lucifer Kills. LK.

I kept at it . . . from the stupid to the sub-
lime . . . from the known to the unknown.
And then it tripped off my tongue—Lord
Kelvin.

Lord Kelvin! I looked down the list. If LK
was Lord Kelvin, then there should be COT—
Cup of Tea. He was there. And Ask Me No
Questions. She was there.

It was a list of abbreviated horse's names
and after each one was the year the calico cat
it had received as a mascot was born.

It was a list of horses that had had Harry's
calico cats as mascots.

I stood up quickly and walked to the window. My arms were folded across my chest. I

knew what Harry had done. The enormity of it . . . the scope of it . . . the sheer intellectual audacity of it was staggering. Harry had, indeed, changed his world. His laughter rolled gently over me. How I missed him!

18

Jo Starobin sat in her rocking char. One Himalayan was on her lap. One was on her shoulder. The others were scattered about, at least one stalking the slow steady rock of the wood.

I was standing behind her. We both watched Detective Senay. He was holding up the piece of taped cardboard.

"Sure," he said, "I looked at it. I looked at it pretty damn carefully."

He held it at arm's length, as if it was something ugly.

"Let me get straight what you're telling me, Mrs. Nestleton."

"I'm not married," I corrected him for the fifth or sixth time.

"What you're saying is this," he continued, brushing aside my objection, his voice rising just up to the limit of anger. "What you're saying is that Harry Starobin was not the sweet kindly man everybody thought he was. He was a kind of magician. He discovered a new way to breed calico cats. He found a way to get a whole slew of calico cats in a single litter because he had these special kinds of barn cats. But that was only the beginning. Not only was he a magician, but these calico cats were magicians also."

He looked at me, arching his eyebrows, grimacing, shuffling his body. The poor man.

He continued. "If one of these calico cats starts to live with a racehorse as the horse's mascot, that broken-down three-legged horse will turn into a champion runner sooner or later."

He stopped again, held out his hands, and asked, "Do I have it right so far?"

"You have it right," I said.

"So Harry began selling these magical calico cats to horse trainers and owners. And he made a lot of money. But we don't know where all that money is, do we?"

Jo looked at me quickly. I said nothing. She knew I had said nothing about the money in her safe-deposit box. I would never say anything about that.

Senay continued. "According to you, what happens next is something like this. Someone wanted this magical line of cats. That someone murdered Harry to obtain them. That someone ripped apart this house to make it seem like a robbery. And that someone killed Mona Aspen and Ginger Mauch because both of them worked with Harry on this scheme. Mona was the one who introduced Harry to the trainers and owners who needed the cats to turn lousy horses into champions. And Ginger was the bagman."

He walked to the sofa and sat down. There was silence for a long time.

Then he grinned. "One of us is crazy, lady. Or, to put it another way, what you told me is very difficult to believe."

I grinned back at him, stiffly. I was not going to let him bait me.

Senay said, "The real problem with stories like these is that when all is said and done, when all the smoke and fire and belief and nonsense clear, there's simply no way to corroborate them."

It was the moment I was waiting for. I knew that Senay would bring up the paucity of demonstrable evidence. I knew that Senay would have to be cornered and recruited, otherwise there would be no chance.

"They can be corroborated," I said quietly.

Senay exploded. "You mean we do a statistical study of racehorses that have calico cats for mascots? Or we subpoena the financial records of every trainer who has a calico cat to see if he paid ten thousand dollars for it when she was a kitten? Who gives a damn whether all that calico-cat nonsense is true or not? I'm investigating murders. Do you understand? Murders." Senay had temporarily lost his cool; he was almost shouting at the end of his little speech.

I handed him a small folded piece of paper. White memo paper.

He opened the paper and read: CALICO KITTENS. NEW LITTER. VERY REASONABLY PRICED. IDEAL

FOR BARN AND STABLE. WRITE: STAROBIN, P.O. BOX 385, OLD BROOKVILLE, LONG ISLAND, NEW YORK.

"I don't understand this," he said. "What is it?"

"An advertisement," I replied, "that, with your consent, will be placed in the classified sections of all the leading thoroughbred racing and breeding magazines."

"But what's the point?"

"Whoever murdered Harry and Mona and Ginger and stole Veronica and her litter will think that there exists another line of magical calico cats. The murderers will find that unacceptable. They will try to get this new litter."

"You mean we create a litter of calico cats?"

"We fake a litter. The litter box will be empty."

"And wait for the thief to show up in the barn?"

"Exactly."

"And the thief is the murderer?"

"Or has been hired by the murderer."

"Did it ever dawn on you, lady, that you have been watching too many Miss Marple mysteries on Channel Thirteen?"

"No. My television set went on the blink two years ago and I never fixed it. But did it ever dawn on you, Detective Senay, that you know absolutely nothing about these murders after all this time—except what I told you today?"

I let that sink in, then continued. "If the killer is truly a madman, and I believe he is

. . . if he is willing to murder to win races . . . then he is not going to let these mythical calico kittens go elsewhere."

He stared at me. I could tell his defenses were beginning to crumble.

"What kind of departmental response are you talking about?" he finally asked.

"Nothing," I replied, "but one police officer at all times in the barn between six in the evening and six in the morning. In plainclothes, in the old hayloft."

"Does it have your approval, Mrs. Starobin?" Senay asked. Then added, "After all, it is your property."

"I suppose so," Jo said.

"Then I'll set the damn thing up," he half-yelled, and strode out of the room as if I had offended him greatly.

When we were alone, the old woman pointed a shaky hand at me and said, "How dare you tell that policeman all those stories about Harry! How can you believe them?"

"You told me yourself, Jo, in the bank, that Harry must have been involved in something criminal. You asked me to help you find out."

"But, Alice, not this . . . not selling kittens for exorbitant prices on the grounds that they make horses champions. It's a fake . . . and Harry wouldn't have had anything to do with it. Harry would have robbed a bank if he was desperate enough—and our financial situation *was* desperate—but not this."

I lowered my voice. I couldn't bear Jo's anguish.

"What if it wasn't a fake, Jo? What if Harry really had bred such a line of kittens? What if all those racehorses began winning suddenly because of their mascots—the calico barn cats . . . what if somehow, in some way, Harry had pulled off a miracle, something that really can't be explained scientifically—what then, Jo?"

Jo didn't answer. She started to weep. The cats seemed to sense her grief and started an orgy of playfulness, as if trying to cheer her up.

Even in springtime the Starobin house was cold and damp in the evening, so Jo and I wore shawls as we spent each evening together, complementing the police officers who split two six-hour shifts in the barn.

I had moved into the cottage again, and slept there, with Pancho and Bushy.

There was a strange enmity between Jo and me—a silent one, as if we had both agreed to a truce in some long-standing struggle.

I didn't understand why Jo avoided speaking to me, or I to her; I didn't understand why the name Harry no longer was mentioned.

Three days after we had begun that evening vigil—after the advertisement had been placed in the six daily and weekly publications and we all waited for a murderous thief to attempt to steal a litter of nonexistent kittens—Jo broke the truce.

She turned on me with a suddenness and a ferocity that made me cringe.

"Don't you think I know what went on between you and Harry?"

I didn't know how to reply. Harry and I had not been lovers. Ginger had been Harry's lover. And she was dead. For all I knew, Mona also had been his long-time secret lover. That might explain her fatal involvement; she might have helped him for love and not for money. And maybe there had been others—maybe there had been hundreds of others. But not I.

Had Jo, in her wisdom, intuited my secret fantasy passion for the old man . . . a strange oedipal passion that I had never articulated to anyone?

I didn't answer. I bowed my head. She construed it as an admission of guilt and she was happy—she forgave me. The air cleared. The hostility dissolved. She mumbled and turned away, making a motion with her hand to signify that it meant nothing.

On the fifth day, as we were keeping vigil in the large house, Jo mentioned that she had spoken to Charlie Coombs and he had asked after me.

"How is Charlie doing?" I asked calmly, academically. It is the proper way to speak about old lovers.

"Okay, I suppose. Did I ever tell you about

his father? His father was a wonderful man. He used to sleep in a stall with a horse if it was sick."

I smiled. I wondered how Charlie Coombs was really doing. Had he bought a new pair of red sneakers? Had he cleaned up his cluttered desk in his small racetrack office? Were his horses winning? Did he miss me? But I could not muse abstracted for long on our affair without that old suspicion beginning to grow again—that Charlie Coombs was part and parcel of the whole mess—that Charlie was on a calico tightrope.

Jo changed the subject: "Should we get coffee for the policemen in the barn?"

"They're being paid," I noted.

"It's been bothering me since the first night they started to stay in the barn. Shouldn't we make them coffee? Amos can do it." Jo was beginning to worry over trifles.

I laughed. "Amos couldn't deliver an empty cup, much less one filled with coffee."

"He's a fine man," Jo leapt to his defense. "It's just that he really wasn't cut out to be a handyman . . . he gets confused."

My mind really wasn't on Amos. I was thinking about what was coming. I was thinking that it would be someone close . . . perhaps Charlie . . . perhaps Nicholas Hill . . . it would be someone I knew who would try to take the nonexistent litter.

I was beginning to experience a profound sense of inadequacy and almost shame, as if, in the face of the bizarre and inexplicable conspiracy of magical cats and triumphant horses created by Harry Starobin, it would be best if the advertisement was ignored . . . it would be best if the guilty would not act and let time dissolve the memories.

"Harry used to love peaches," Jo said, startling me with a comment that had nothing to do with anything. "We used to buy bushels of hard unripe peaches on the roadside in front of the Mannigalt farm."

It dawned on me that Jo was probably speaking about a farm that had closed its doors twenty years ago. She was talking about a Long Island that had long since vanished.

On the eighth day, at ten-thirty in the evening, Jo began to act strange again. We had nothing to do but play rummy together. Two or three letters had dribbled in about the nonexistent kittens and there had been a few phone calls. But the barn was still inviolable.

Suddenly Jo whispered, "Why calico?"

"What?"

"If what you say is true, Alice, if Harry did what you said he did . . . why did he breed calicos?"

"I don't follow you, Jo."

"Why not seal point or red tabby or silver mackerel? And why a short-haired barn cat? Why not a Persian or a Manx or a Maine coon or a Himalayan?"

Her questions were becoming hysterical.

"Calm down," I said, gently but firmly re-seating her.

Then I said, "Maybe he thought calicos were special. Maybe he loved them because they were so hard to breed."

"Harry never told me that," Jo said, her voice rising again.

I tried to be rational. "I don't think he knew about their special qualities until Cup of Tea. I think he just bred calicos at first because he wanted to show that he knew more about cats than the people who wrote books about them. He wanted to do things that people said he couldn't do."

Jo picked up the cards again and started to play. She kept nodding her head and forming words with her lips—mutely, as if she was carrying on a very important internal conversation.

Then she stared at me and said, "Ashes."

"What do you mean, Jo?"

"Ashes. Our marriage was ashes. It turned out in the end to be ashes."

"He did it for you, Jo—for the money, for the house, for the way you lived, for you, Jo, and what you had been to each other all those years." I don't know why I said that. I didn't believe it. If he did it for anyone other than himself, it was Ginger or Mona. But that was too sad to speak.

"It's all over. And it's all ashes. Just like Harry's ashes on the gravel roadway," Jo said, and her body began to be racked with chills. I wrapped a blanket around her.

I was beginning to intuit that whatever else was going on, we were performing a wake for Harry Starobin. The old man had burned his own peculiar life in each of us. He was a lover, husband, father, breeder, Merlin. A bizarre man none of us really knew in the end.

I closed my eyes. I could see him rising from the ashes of the roadway—funny, potent, sad, compassionate, inquisitive. And, above all, wise. Was it his supposed wisdom that so infatuated all of us, why we still hung on to his memory like drowning people?

I wanted to leave the house. I wanted to talk to Bushy and Pancho in the cottage. They didn't like it there.

"If you don't mind, I'll turn in before the curfew, Jo." It had been decided that we would stay together in the living room of the house from the moment it got dark until midnight, and then leave the vigil to the police officers hiding in the barn loft.

Jo nodded. It was fine with her. I left quickly and walked back to the cottage. Poor Pancho. Poor Bushy. All alone in a strange cottage again.

I had just reached the door of the cottage when a scream split the night air.

And then a crack, as if something had been broken in a sound chamber.

I turned, petrified.

I saw lights switching on in the large house and the barn.

Jo was walking toward the barn as fast as she could.

I started to run.

When I reached the barn I saw the police officer crouched against the barn door, blood streaming from a wound on the side of his head. His gun was drawn. He seemed crazed, disoriented.

He shouted at Jo, who was pressing what seemed to be a dish towel against his wound: "I got him! He hit me with a flashlight! But I got him!"

I could now see blood all around in the flickering lights. Blood on the officer. Blood on the barn door. And a trail of red blotches leading from the barn into the overgrown field, as if someone had placed red doilies on the ground.

"Get him," the officer pleaded, unsteady. "He's hurt bad. Get him!"

Jo and I walked into the field, holding each other. Then we stopped. Where were we going? It was dark. How could we find him? What would we do if we did find him?

We huddled together. We waited. We stared back at the barn lights.

Something came to us on the night breeze.

It sounded like a cricket. No, it sounded like a night warbler.

No, it was a human sound. A moan. At first we thought it was the wounded policeman, but he was too far away.

We moved toward it, our shoulders touching.

Now we could see something alien in the grass; a heap.

Jo's foot kicked something metallic.

"Flashlight," she whispered.

I picked it up and flicked it on, grabbing Jo's hand with my own free hand.

The heap was a body. Alive. Knees brought up to the chest in pain. A blood-soaked thigh.

We moved closer.

It wasn't a man. It was a woman. The beam of the flashlight was full force on her face.

I stared in horror at her writhing.

My legs could no longer hold my body. I sank beside her.

I placed my hand on the face of my old friend—Carla Fried.

Then there were sirens. And feet crashing through the field.

People surrounded us, loaded the woman on an aluminum rack, and wheeled her out of the field.

Senay helped me up. Jo was hanging on to a uniformed policeman. I felt affection for Senay—an impossible-to-explain affection.

I said to him very slowly and precisely, "The man who sent her . . . the man who sent others to murder . . . the man who now has the barn cat Veronica and her calico litter . . . is a Canadian millionaire named Thomas Waring."

Senay said, "Yes, I've heard the name."

I added, "He's also a patron of the arts," and

then began to laugh hysterically at the dirty little joke. But the laughter died in my throat when I saw someone wrap a blanket around Jo and lead her very slowly and very tentatively out of the field. I was suddenly frightened that she would have to walk over Harry's ashes to reach the house.

19

"How is Mrs. Starobin?" Senay asked.

"Fine. She's fine."

I sat down on the sofa. Jo was upstairs, tucked into bed and sleeping. The first rays of morning sun were beginning to filter through the house.

In front of the rocking chair on which Detective Senay sat was a large paper bag. He reached in, brought out a container of coffee, leaned over, and handed it to me.

Three of the Himalayan cats quickly surrounded the paper bag and inspected it carefully.

"This is out of my own pocket," he noted ruefully.

Then he reached into the bag again and came out with a toasted corn muffin wrapped in aluminum foil. He handed that to me also.

It was, I suppose, the only way Detective Senay could apologize to me for his past behavior toward me. I wanted to be gracious. I was too exhausted to be anything else.

We sipped our coffee, nibbled our muffins,

and stared at each other and at the Himalayans.

Finally he said, "So this woman Carla Fried is a good friend of yours."

"An old friend," I replied.

"Well," he noted, "if she lives, which she probably will, she'll cut a deal. All she has to do is name her associates—she couldn't have murdered Starobin and Mona Aspen and the young girl alone. And then finger that Canadian, Waring, as the man who pulled all the strings. When all the smoke clears, she'll end up doing five years .. if that."

"How can we be sure she'll talk?" I asked.

"Simple. If she doesn't, we'll hang an attempted-murder charge against her for attacking the cop in the barn. No, your friend will play ball with us. She has no other option."

He finished his coffee, crushed the container, and dropped it down beside the paper bag for the cats to play with.

Then he straightened up on the chair. "What's right is right. You did a helluva job, lady. You broke the case."

I didn't respond. He grinned and added, "To be honest, when you set up that calico-kitten trap, I thought you were a stone lunatic."

He was starting to squirm. Poor Senay.

I closed my eyes. He was right. I had broken the case. But never in my wildest dreams had I suspected Carla Fried.

She had pulled the wool over my eyes completely. I had thought she was visiting me and calling me only because of the part, or because we were old friends . . . but in fact, she was in New York to orchestrate a different kind of drama—murder and theft for her patron.

I had thought she was flying in and out of New York, but all the while she was probably in town, keeping tabs on things, telling her associates just when it was the right time to run her old friend down with a red pickup truck because she was getting too inquisitive.

And I really had no idea why she had done it. Had it been a quid pro quo? Had Waring said: I'll give you 1.5 million dollars for your theater if you do something for me? Or had Waring and she been lovers?

Had the promise of a well-funded independent theater company been so important to Carla that she would participate in murder?

How could she, in fact, have anything to do with a man who was so obviously obsessed with winning at all costs—even horse races?

Why? Why? Why? What made Carla run? Passion? Ambition? The promise of artistic freedom? A whim? Psychosis? All of the above?

The more I thought about it, the more I had to face the nagging, hard-to-accept, but harder-to-deny possibility that Carla Fried was just another talented woman who had been crushed to death by theatrical fantasies . . . who had become so deranged and so confused by the need to achieve something in the theater that she would do anything to fulfill that need. Anything!

"You know," Senay said quietly, "your crazy friend probably didn't even know Harry Starobin or Mona Aspen or Ginger Mauch."

I opened my eyes. He was right. And that was the most pernicious and ugly fact of all.

As for Waring! How obsessed with winning he must have become. And how twisted. With his money, he could have bought the cats from Harry, like others had. But no! Waring had to be the sole possessor of the cats. He had to guarantee exclusivity by having Harry and Mona and Ginger murdered. He had to relish the sense of secret power as his thoroughbreds began to win ... and only he would know the reason why. His wealth had not brought him virtue or wisdom. It had turned him into a murderous, psychotic fool.

"Maybe she didn't even like cats," Senay added.

"She liked my cats."

"Do you have calico cats?"

"No."

I stared out the front window of the Starobin house. Amos, the old handyman, was walking slowly up the drive. I shivered and reached for one of the blankets on the sofa. Amos was walking over Harry Starobin's ashes.

"How about another muffin?" Senay asked, reaching down into the paper bag.

"No thanks."

"Danish, then?"

"No thanks."

Senay sighed wearily and commenced to rock.

The Himalayans abandoned the paper bag. They had found nothing of value there.

Amos walked into the house, through the large living room, and into the kitchen. He didn't greet us.

I heard all the Himalayans moving toward him. They were hungry. I heard him preparing their food. Before I fell asleep on the sofa I remember thinking that they sure feed cats early in Old Brookville.

20

I opened the cat carriers the moment I closed the apartment door behind me.

Bushy ambled out. Pancho flew out to begin his frantic dashes in order to find, identify, and flee from the many enemies which had invaded Manhattan while he was away.

I walked into the kitchen, opened the refrigerator, took out a container of low-fat milk, and poured myself half a glass. I sat down at the tiny table. My body felt as if all the musculature had been sucked out.

The green light on the phone machine indicated there had been messages while I was away. Pancho's enemies. I ignored them.

I sipped the milk. My hands were shaking. I was becoming agitated.

Reaching for pencil and pad, I made a soothing list:

1. Pick up hat left in bar
2. Write nice note to Charlie Coombs
3. Call Anthony Basillio and thank him again
4. Buy saffron rice for Pancho

5. Cash check
6. Buy toothpaste and regular cat food

I put the pencil down. It was musty in the apartment. I left the kitchen and walked to the windows in the living room—heaving both of them open as far as the cracked wood allowed.

Turning back, I saw the paperback copy of *Romeo and Juliet* on the long table.

Poor Carla Fried, willing to do anything for anyone to fund her dream of a theater. Poor, sick, crazed Carla.

I went back to the kitchen to finish my milk.

Strange thoughts came to me as I sat there.

What if Carla's theater group in Montreal had already been funded?

What if, in spite of the fact that Thomas Waring and his associates would be convicted of murder, the funds were already in place, in possession of the theater group, inviolate?

What if the season would go on as planned . . . without Carla Fried . . . without Thomas Waring?

What if they would still need an actress to imaginatively interpret the role of the Nurse in a Portobello production of *Romeo and Juliet?*

I picked up the pencil and added another item to the list:

7. Contact Carla's theatrical group in Montreal

A part is a part, I said to myself grimly.

And Portobello would appreciate my interpretation of the Nurse as a middle-aged woman whose eccentricities hid the fact that she loved Romeo just as passionately as Juliet loved him. Portobello would find the idea intriguing . . . chewable . . . dramaturgically innovative.

"I'll discuss it in detail with Bushy before I discuss it with Portobello," I said to the pencil in my hand. Then I walked into the living room to join Bushy on the sofa.

The woman whose name was Francesca Tosques, and was vaguely attached to the Italian legation, had told me before I started the cat sitting assignment that Geronimo was a lovely cat but he had some peculiarities.

"Don't go near the fireplace," she said mysteriously. "Fine," I replied. Francesca was going to be away for three days: Sunday, Monday, and Tuesday. All I had to do was go up to her large old apartment on West End Avenue and Ninety-seventh Street in Manhattan, feed Geronimo, talk to Geronimo, kill some time. That's all. A rather good assignment as far as these things go.

I arrived on Sunday at three in the afternoon after walking all the way from my East Twenty-sixth Street apartment through the park. It was hot outside but the apartment was cool, utilizing only one large slow ceiling fan. The view from the apartment was spectacular out over the Hudson to Jersey, north up the Hudson, downtown. Pick a window, pick a view. She had left me twenty-three notes on the dining room table complicating the simplest procedures. But I was used to that.

As for Geronimo—I was expecting a Balinese or a Cornish Rex or some other exotic feline but when I finally met him, he was lying on the formica kitchen table, well, Geronimo was simply an old fashioned black alley cat. You couldn't call him anything else. He was big and brawny and ugly with scars up and down his flanks and he walked, when he did walk, like alley cats do—as if he had some kind of testicular problem, to put it kindly.

That first day I stayed in the apartment for about an hour talking to Geronimo, who really wasn't listening. After eating he had gone back to the formica table and I had to almost shout to get my points across. I joshed him, telling him that I was a famous actress, a famous sleuth, and above all, a famous cat sitter and I'd be damned if he was going to be standoffish. I just wouldn't tolerate it.

On the third day, we still weren't any friendlier; it was live and let live. Anyway, on that last day of the assignment, Geronimo was beginning to irritate me. My pride was hurt. Everyone always said I had a magical way with cats. Ask my own cats—Bushy and Pancho—they'll tell anyone. What Francesca had told me had really started to bother me—that I should not go near the fireplace. Very strange. The fireplace was old and large, set in the north wall of the apartment. It was obviously a working one but it was also obvious that it hadn't been used in a long time. I had kept away from it because of what she had told me, and because it was in a far part of the apartment. I mean, one really had to want to go there to end up there. So, I sat and stewed at the living room table staring at Geronimo, who was staring at me. Instead of a forty-one-year-old woman, I was thinking like a twelve-year-old adolescent. Something had been denied me. Authority had spoken. It was necessary to subvert authority. It was a decidedly adolescent impulse.

I got up slowly, theatrically, elegantly, and sauntered over to the fireplace. Reaching it, I placed one hand gently on the mantlepiece and smiled.

A moment later a blur exploded across the room. And then I felt a short intense pain in the thumb of the hand resting on the fireplace.

Startled, I looked down. Geronimo was standing there. He had flown across the room and bit me. Can you imagine that?

Then he just turned and sauntered back towards the kitchen table, very much the macho alley cat.

In a state of semi-shock from the attack, I stumbled into the bathroom and ran water to clean the small wound. Geronimo stared at me from his kitchen table, bored, inferring that I had been duly warned and that since I had obviously wanted to play with fire, it was simple justice that I got burned.

After I washed and dressed the wound I felt a need to recuperate. I walked into Francesca's bedroom and lay down on the bed, closed my eyes and flicked on the radio. The station was set on 1010 WINS—news all day, every day.

I lay there, wondering why Geronimo attacked people who stood in front of the fireplace. It was very perplexing. I must have dozed off because I awoke with a start. My mouth was dry. A bad dream? No. A name on the radio was being repeated that I recognized. The announcer was saying that one of the last famous Greenwich Village bohemians was dead. Arkavy Reynolds had been shot to death on Jane Street. Reynolds, the announcer said, was a well-known denizen of the lower Manhattan theatrical scene. He was the producer and publisher of a theatrical scandal shreet that he hawked himself from coffee shop to coffee shop, and one of those outrageous individuals who was at one time so much a part of bohemian life in New York. The announcer ended with the comment that the police were investigating the murder but have no leads or witnesses at this time.

Poor Arkavy! I bumped into him often over the years and we always chatted, or rather I listened to his monologue. He was a huge fat man who seemed to roll down the street. In all seasons he wore the same outfit: a cab driver's hat, white shirt and flamboyant tie, vest, farmer's overalls with shoulder straps, and construction worker shoes. Of course, he was quite mad. Rumor had it that he came from a wealthy family. He was always looking for space to perform some play, far off off Broadway. He was always talking about some brilliant new playwright whom no one ever heard of. And his newsletters were often about people that simply didn't exist. Each issue of his newsletter also carried reviews written by him, which were filled with typographical excesses—he loved asterisks and exclamation marks and dots and dashes.

I got up from the bed and walked into the kitchen. There was Geronimo. He no longer interested me at all. I ignored him. I absent-mindedly opened and closed the refrigerator a few times, thinking of Arkavy, trying to remember the exact time I saw him last. It might have been on East Fourth Street and First Avenue one night in the fall of 1989. I was going to a drama reading by an East German woman. Yes, it might have been then.

I left the kitchen and walked back into the living room where I fell wearily into a chair. My wound was beginning to throb. Geronimo was still looking at me. It dawned on me, right then, that if Arkavy and Geronimo had by chance met, they might have become the best of friends. After all, poor Arkavy was a man who spent his life looking to be bitten.

And now someone had killed him.